GETTING OVER MAX COOPER

MARCELLE KARP

GETTING
OVER
MAX
COOPER

putnam

G. P. PUTNAM'S SONS

G. P. PUTNAM'S SONS
An imprint of Penguin Random House LLC, New York

First published in the United States of America by G. P. Putnam's Sons,
an imprint of Penguin Random House LLC, 2022

G. P. Putnam's Sons is a registered trademark of Penguin Random House LLC.

Visit us online at penguinrandomhouse.com

Library of Congress Cataloging-in-Publication Data is available.

Printed in the United States of America

ISBN 9780593325049

1 3 5 7 9 10 8 6 4 2

LSCH

Design by Nicole Rheingans
Text set in Warnock Pro

This book is a work of fiction. Any references to historical events, real people,
or real places are used fictitiously. Other names, characters, places, and events
are products of the author's imagination, and any resemblance to actual events
or places or persons, living or dead, is entirely coincidental.

For Ruby

The Beginning
of Summer

Chapter One

"Can you get off your phone, Jazz? We got customers here," Sue barks at me, her high-pitched voice in surround sound as she nudges me off the stool with her hip, here in the way, way back of Crabby's.

"Yeah, okay," I mutter. I was literally sitting for one minute; I'd been watching Ariana Grande's video "Thank U, Next," the historical *Mean Girls* version, an epic mash-up of my favorite singer becoming a character from one of my favorite movies.

"Also, Jazz, I need you to use the disinfectant every single time you wipe the counter down," she says, invading my personal space with her breath, which is a combination of coffee and cigarettes and weed. "Everything needs to be sanitized, got me?"

As if I don't already know that. Still, I don't answer her with what I'd like to say ("Shut up, shut up, shut up") because she's the boss. I put my iPhone in the back pocket of my denim skirt, adjust my sweaty purple tank top, then grab the spray, squirting the air like I'm perfuming it as I walk toward the counter of this shoe box of a snack shack that is my summer job.

"Move it, move it," orders Nate Beckerman, sounding like a drill sergeant, his intonation clipped. He doesn't speak that way naturally; he is a high school student like me, but Nate wants to be an actor, so he's always doing what he calls "character work." I guess he's in military mode right now.

"At your command!" I laugh, saluting him.

Nate acknowledges my salute with a nod of his chin as he leans over the counter and grabs a peppermint patty from the plastic bin that's next to my cash register. It costs twenty-five cents, but he just takes it like he owns Crabby's. A blatant consequence of his privilege. Sue is going to be pissed if she catches him—I am under orders to charge *everyone* for *everything*. Even my mom pays.

I squirt Nate with disinfectant, as if he's a mosquito I'm spritzing with repellent. "Can you stop? I'm going to get in trouble," I whine, then quickly modulate my voice, trying to sound normal, as I realize Nate's cousin McDimple (his actual name is Leo) is standing off to the side of my counter. The top half of McDimple's wet suit is dangling off his hip bones, his body is damp from the ocean, and he's on his phone, a 'droid—who has a 'droid other than moms? "What, um, what do you want, Nate?"

"Ice cream, B!" I know what the *B* stands for, and I am not here for it.

"You're going to have to try that again," I tell him rather sternly.

McDimple looks up from his phone and catches me staring, then smiles, flashing his dimples, and they momentarily blind me before I return to earth.

"Can I get a Rocky Road, please?" McDimple asks as he glides to Nate's side, phone in hand, elbows on my counter, dimples winking. Does McDimple wake up in the morning and bask in his exquisiteness? I would if I had those thick black eyelashes, those green eyes that twinkle, and those lips—ah, those lips. "This dork will have the same."

"Yo, earth to Jazz?" Nate pushes my shoulder gently, laughing as he busts me zoning out at McDimple. He has the biggest mop of curly black hair of the century, and it bounces with every step, every movement of his arms; it's so comical it makes it hard to stay mad at him for very long.

"Sugar cone or wafer?" I ask. There are no customers behind Nate and McDimple, we are slow, slow, slow. Soon, like once we hit the Fourth of July, I'll be busy all the time here in this sweatbox, serving people ice cream and their basic iced coffees, having to explain over and over again that we don't make lattes.

"You decide for me," McDimple says, and what he really means is: *Okay, Jasmine, you can kiss me now.* McDimple is the unicorn of boys: new here, attractive. I want him to be my Valentine. Chill, with wavy dark hair. Fit, with skin that glistens like Edward Cullen's. Wears T-shirts of indie bands from the '90s, with names like Pavement and Lush and Hole that I've had to google, music I don't listen to at all. Doesn't walk around with AirPods in his ears. All things I've picked up from simply observing him for the last five days that I've been back in Fair Harbor.

Quite possibly cuffed. I only have this impression because I did see him with an impossibly beautiful redheaded girl at Max Cooper's free Friday night. Still. Even if he's taken, I can allow myself the luxury of appreciating his beauty.

"Sprinkles?" I don't have empirical data on this, but I do know that people like sprinkles. Especially kids—they like everything that is a possibly messy situation.

"Seriously, Jazz, any more questions?" Nate says impatiently, back in his Nate voice.

"Um, excuse me, Nate, but if I don't ask the questions now, you'll ask me for sprinkles later."

"Ohhh, the sprinkle police are here, everybody—"

"Hey, Nate, chill," McDimple interrupts Nate and the noise stops.

A gasp slips from my throat. It's very possible this is the moment when I fall in love with McDimple. Normally I don't condone the actions of a King T'Challa protecting me, a woman, but I'll let him have this one. It's a rush, actually, and I'm so overwhelmed that my whole face becomes a furnace.

I hurl my upper body into the freezer, sugar cones in my left hand, while I scoop, or rather dig, at the frozen tundra of ice cream. I am supposed to warm up the scooper and scoop the ice cream in an *S* pattern, but I can't focus; I have McDimple rolling under my skin, and I stab at the thick, milky ice, unable to concentrate on formations.

Sue puts her hand on my back, startling me out from the cool air of the freezer's innards. I stand up, ice cream cones filled now with Rocky Road. They're not the smoothest scoops I've ever captured, and have triple the amount of ice cream Sue allows for a double scoop, but I'm not going to stress about it.

"Just checking to see whether you've fallen in," she says, her eyebrow clocking the scoop mountains in my hands, her blue bandana holding her frizzy hair away from her overtanned face. She could be twenty-five or fifty-five—I have no idea; she just reads old to me.

As I head back to the counter, McDimple has a camera out, a pocket Hasselblad—a very important brand of camera for photographers of all levels—and he's pointing it at me. The camera is a goal of mine. To own one, that is. I have so many questions for him: Is he a photographer? Is this a camera he owns? What is happening right now?

Because: if he is a photographer, I absolutely *should* know him. Taking photos is what I want to do for a living when I escape high school. Lots of my friends take photos of themselves and lots of my friends post cool shots on their Instagrams, but for me, photography is a way to tell stories.

Backup plan: master feminism and then teach it.

"What . . ." I say instead. Words: not my forte, ever. However, I'd get an A+ in awkward any day of the week.

"We're going to surf by Birch. Adera and them are out there now," Nate tells me as he pays for the cones and hands one to McDimple. Adera MacIntosh is another girl in our friend group, and the universal use of "them" means probably Kim Chang and Gus Stuto, other mainstays of our group, who don't have day jobs like me. "You gonna come after work?"

Birch is the beach we all hang out on. We refer to it as Birch because the pathway to that part of the beach is via Birch Walk, which is the walk Macy Whelan, my best friend, lives on. A long time ago, when our moms and babysitters and dads dictated where and how we spent our days, Birch was where they met so the kids could have playdates while the adults on duty drank in the sun. And even though the parents don't hover around us anymore, Birch is still our spot.

"Maybe. Macy is coming back today, so it'll depend on what she wants to do." For me, there is no summer without Macy; this is where we've spent our childhood riding our boogie boards in the surf and climbing up the stairs of the lighthouse and lying in the sun on the floating raft in the bay. Macy hasn't been here in two weeks; she and her bouncy-castle nine-year-old brother, Dylan, were doing required time with their dad, Dr. Anthony Whelan, who, because he hates Macy's mom, Olive, refuses to come to Fire Island, even though Macy and Dylan love being here.

"Which ferry?" McDimple asks, still behind the camera. I am trying to avoid further descent into awkward by not posing, and instead, focus on how McDimple and I are connecting about ferries.

"No clue—she's been annoyingly vague about her arrival." I turn to see where Sue is, nervous that she'll yell at me for having the tiniest amount of fun. But she's not in sight; maybe she's in the bathroom or in outer space, anywhere that's not here.

"Come on, bro, stop taking pictures of her," Nate says to McDimple, smacking him on the arm. "Don't take it personally, Jazz, he shoots everyone. All you photographers are the same. Okay, we out."

McDimple lowers the camera from his face and raises his thick eyebrows at me, essentially asking me to marry him, but maybe not, and then he says, "Later."

I lean forward on the counter, almost stretching, watching them chatter as they move away from my daydream with a deliberate pace. Ahead of them is tranquility: the glassine Great South Bay of Long Island, dotted with docked boats and puttering ferries.

"Hey, lady, if you lean on my counter like that, you're going to crack it," Sue says, now having reappeared from whatever upside-down world she'd been lurking in.

I turn, wishing I could talk to her about what just happened. But. She's not my friend, she's my boss. And also:

I just had an almost-conversation with the cutest boy in the whole world, our very first since I arrived. Oh, sure, he's come to Crabby's to order things, but this was the first time where we had actually exchanged words instead of just looking at each other.

And that is enough to make my day.

● ● ●

This is my summer life so far in Fair Harbor, at my day job as the best ice cream scooper in all of Fire Island (with the exception of my dual Rocky Road disaster cones just now) and my friends stopping by to give me updates about where they'll be and when, which I appreciate, because it helps to know where to go after work. Mom and I have been coming to this specific town for fourteen of my sixteen summers, trading city life for beach life. Fire Island is only an hour and ten minutes away from Manhattan by the Long Island Rail Road, with a bonus half-hour ride on the ferry that glides across the Great South Bay, delivering you to the town of your choice; there are seventeen distinct communities along these thirty-three miles of barrier island. There's the Pines and Cherry Grove, which are the safest of havens for the LGBTQ community, and there's Ocean Beach, which is filled with the yearlong locals plus a whole bunch of restaurants and shops and a school, and there's even a town called Point O' Woods that you need a key to enter. And my town? My town is where housewives wade around in ginormous sun hats, and over-tanned dad bods stand at the dock with fishing rods, and kids ride their bikes without helmets. You get on the ferry on the mainland and you leave Americuh behind you; all that's here is everything that is summer.

Crabby's, where I work, is part of the grocery store, Woodson's. It's like Woodson's is the main house, and Crabby's is its tiny garage. To enter or exit Crabby's, you have to walk through Woodson's, and even the bathroom is in Woodson's, which is where Sue disappeared to. And so I use these twelve seconds of Sue-free time to text with Adera—she wants me to take some shots of her with my camera for her Insta today.

> Meet me at my house at 5:30

She responds with a thumbs-up. She's hit me up almost every day since I've been back to take glam shots for her Insta, and I don't mind, as long as she gives me credit; she's got like twelve hundred Instagram followers, so that's free promotion for me, budding photographer.

"Jasmine Jacobsoooooooon!" That voice, it comes from around that corner where McDimple and Nate turned right and disappeared. Which means:

OH MY GOD, IT'S MACY! SHE'S HERE.

"Macyyyyyy!" It's the best surprise, and I'm not even mad that she didn't text me that she was on the ferry.

Summer can begin now.

We both scream at the same time—not words, just sounds of joy. Sue is throwing me shade because she does not get the experience of joy, and we're hugging each other over this dumb counter, me barely reaching Macy—I'm just so short—and she smells like vanilla ice cream. I don't take hugs for granted anymore. I give them and accept them readily.

"I love the way this color is looking, Jazz," Macy says, touching the pink stripes cutting through my brown hair.

"I'm going to need you to do touch-ups," I tell her. The thing about coloring my dark brown hair is that I need to constantly replenish it. Every wash, every time I go out into the sun, it fades just a little bit, enough for it not to look the way I want it to, which is vibrant and *pink*.

"You know I love playing colorist." She laughs as she runs a hand through her long blond hair; she's been helping me keep my pink highlights ever since I started doing them when I was twelve.

"I'm so happy to see you, Moo," I say, using our pet name for each other.

"Me too!" She leans back over the counter and pulls my forehead to hers. "I've *missed* you."

We haven't had many sleepovers this year—the last time we did was for my birthday in March when Macy came to New York City for two days and Mom gave me her credit card and let us go to a fancy restaurant without her. We haven't texted much; we FaceTime mostly, but even that has been sporadic.

I am so happy to have my person back.

"Allo, Jazzy!" Standing right behind Macy is Gayle, their nanny since forever—first she was Macy's, and now she watches Dylan, who needs full-time supervision. Plus, Olive can't do the parenting part during the week because she has a job in Philadelphia, where they live. And the dad only sees them once a month, for a weekend, which isn't even partial parenting; that's visiting with some kids that happen to be yours.

"Hi, Gayle!" I say, releasing Macy, who is resplendent in her denim strapless romper and flip-flops, her arms sculpted, unlike the baby bat wings I flap about. Macy's on the lacrosse team at her school, which I suppose is the benefit of going to school in the suburbs of Philadelphia—they have land and space to do actual sports, unlike my high school, where we just have an indoor gym.

"You think I could order an ice cream cone, love? Mint chocolate chip?" Gayle says. She's British, with the kind of eyes that give her the air of a woman with a permanent smile on her big moon-shaped face, and I can never tell if that's just her face or if it's in fact how she is: a happy person. "Dylan, would you like a cone?"

Dylan is doing cartwheels in front of Crabby's, and it's possible he hasn't heard Gayle. She asks him one more time if he wants a cone of something, anything, and he shrugs, so we take it as a no. He is so annoying, this kid. "Macy? Interested?"

"I'm good, G," Macy says, taking a selfie, with me in the far background bent over the ice cream freezer. If my arms don't turn into world championship bodybuilder arms by the end of the summer, I will be surprised, because ice cream scooping is a grind.

"Dude, why didn't you text me you were on the ferry?!" I yell to Macy as I emerge from the ice vortex. I promptly get woozy, hold the freezer for balance, and then, when I'm settled, approach the counter, taking a swig of water, because hydration.

"I wanted to surprise you," Macy says as she takes the cone from me and hands it to Gayle. Gayle sits on the bench that is between Woodson's and Crabby's to eat her ice cream, and Dylan sits next her, in his denim shorts and oversized Kaepernick sleeveless football jersey, rambling about whatever it is that nine-year-old boys care about. "Plus, Max was on the ferry, so you know . . ."

Macy's "you know" is code for *I saw Max Cooper and I am so happy right now*. Max Cooper was her non-boyfriend

boyfriend last summer, and we thought he liked Macy as much as she liked him until after the fourth time they had sex and he started ghosting her. The sex part was a big deal because she had never done it before, but the way he treated her was the worst part. There was a rumor he gave her COVID, but he didn't, she was just heartsick and couldn't get out of bed for almost all of August. According to every single thing I know about Macy, he's the first boy she's really fallen for.

"And?"

"It was like we've always known each other. He was so chatty and—"

"Girls, I hate to break up this lovefest, but we are working. Unless you're buying, you need to go bye-bye," Sue says.

Gayle, done with her ice cream cone, interrupts us with her ever-present haughty tone. "Macy, let's go home and you can see your little friend later, right?"

Dylan jumps in the air, fist-pumping, psyched to be off the bench and on his way home.

Macy rolls her eyes and looks at Gayle. "Okay, *fine*." Macy leans in with that long torso of hers, gives me a big hug, and then she's gone.

I want to spend every second with Macy Whelan now that she's back in Fair Harbor. The school year plus Macy living in Philadelphia and me living in Manhattan has kept us from doing what we love: riding our bikes from our town to the lighthouse in Kismet, and being in a water taxi, our arms dangling off the back of the boat, the spray of the ocean nipping at our fingertips, and going to the dock at sunset and watching the sky turn from blue to pink to dark violet. Because all of that and so much more can only happen here in Fair Harbor with my best friend for life, Macy Whelan.

• • •

Hands down, the most gorgeous group of girls I have ever seen in person are my next customers, walking up to the counter as Macy and Gayle and Dylan leave. Clearly, they've just gotten off the ferry that Macy was on. There are four of them, each as pretty as the others, pulling their wheelie luggage, ooohing and aaahing at the lone deer walking past Crabby's, as if they've never been in nature. Also, we can't pet or feed the deer because of ticks: those bloodsuckers cling to the deer that populate this island, and it's a problem we have to be wary of.

But the one that has me speechless is the lanky one with the long vibrant ginger hair and ice-blue eyes whose face was plastered to Leo's at Max Cooper's on Friday night.

"You an Ariana stan?" she asks, her eyes dripping dark judgment. I look down at my chest, momentarily spacing on what I'd put on today: Ari's *Sweetener* T-shirt with the purple camo background. The burn vibrates, and I'm not sure if it's because she's making fun of me or if it's because I feel that familiar jealousy of a girl who captures the attention of a boy that I pine for. She leans against my counter, as her friends stand in the middle of Broadway, talking about how cute this place is. "Like, modern much?"

She just dissed me, *to my face.* Not cool. Not cool at all.

"I'm sorry. Do we have a problem?"

Her face scrunches up; clearly, she is not appreciating my ability to speak up for myself. "I just want four iced coffees. No sugar. Actually, can you give me a few sugar packets? And one of those coffees, I want it to be half milk, half decaf. Good?" She spins around and, with her back to me, calls to one of her friends.

"Sekiya, did you say iced coffee or iced tea?"

A girl with thick crimson passion braids and tattered short-shorts lifts her bedazzled pink oval sunglasses and replies that she wants iced tea, her caramel skin sparkling in the sun. So that's Sekiya. I need to find her Instagram—it will require a little detective work—and find out her story. She personi-fies cool to me. Is she a model too, or is "Beauty" simply her middle name?

The main girl spins back around. "Never mind. Three iced coffees, one iced tea..." She is interrupted as her friends crowd around her, and they are talking about a fashion show one of them had to be at (Working? In the audience? I can't tell). They don't seem to mind that they interrupt one another or that no one can finish a sentence, and I am moving as quickly as I can to make their drinks as I see the line of customers start to grow.

These girls probably have boys hitting them up on Snap and TikTok, and I would put money on it that they're popular and I wouldn't be surprised if they already owned everything I would love to buy at Sephora. I will never know what it is like to exist in the world the way they do, never stressing about a chin hair or back fat or being invisible.

"That's eighteen dollars," I tell the kissing-Leo-McDimple-one as I place the drink carrier on the counter. She hands me her credit card, this sleek blue metal thing, ALICE ADAMS embossed on its face. Now I can find her on Instagram; if they're together, she might have a post about him or something.

Alice waits for me to finishing ringing her up, takes her card back, picks up the tray, turns her back to me as her friends crowd around, and says, "Okay, bitches, slurpy time!"

They are standing right in front of her. Why yell?

I am exhausted by the time they leave my counter. I glance at my phone. I have a few hours of work left, and those hours seem like three days away.

•　•　•

In addition to sanitizing the counter and other things I touch, my day includes answering the phone ("No, sorry, we don't do delivery." How hard is it for people to leave their houses to get their iced coffees?). Sometimes, when it's really, really slow, I count how many people walk by Crabby's; I once was able to count eighty-two consecutive people before one interrupted

the streak by walking up to my counter and ordering something to eat. Ah, the joys of a summer job.

"Hey, Jazz," Max Cooper says, interrupting my lack of motion, wearing his uniform of an oversized white T-shirt and baggy shorts and flip-flops, and even though he's a giant in my mind, this perpetrator of breaking Macy's heart, he's actually more like Hobbit size. He's not a big dude, and while I personally don't find him attractive, I'd think he was hot if I didn't know what a jerk he is.

"What do you want?" I ask, bitchier than I am in real life, fire coming out of every orifice. Max Cooper feels my fury, and it singes his blond eyebrows. I don't care that he was nice to Macy on the ferry; I know how much he hurt her last summer.

Max Cooper leans across the counter so his face is close to mine, and he smiles, his blue eyes sparkling, going for that vampiric charm, I guess, by luring me into his gaze. He's used to girls swooning over him, but I'm not one of them.

"I actually wanted to talk to you, Jazz, about Macy."

While I want to know why he was on the Fair Harbor ferry instead of the Saltaire one, and I want to know why he's in front of me right now, I do *not* want to speak with him about anything outside of what he orders. I mean, the ice cream is better in Saltaire, where he lives: it's actual gelato.

Sue barks at Max Cooper not to lean on the counter, and because she's an adult, he morphs into a Boy Scout.

Marcelle Karp

"Yeah, yeah, sorry, ma'am," he calls out to Sue, and then he looks to me. "Can I get a lobster roll?"

"You *know* we don't make lobster rolls," I snap. "If you don't know what you want, you're going to have to move so I can take care of the next customer."

Max Cooper turns and now sees what I already know: there are no customers behind him.

"Okay, I want . . . a mint chocolate chip, three scoops."

"Sugar or wafer cone?"

"Did you have fun the other night?" Max Cooper asks as he points to the wafer cone.

Yes, I did have fun at his party last weekend. I saw the most beautiful boy in the world, Leo McDimple. And I watched Max Cooper mash with a girl who did not resemble the Very Serious Girlfriend that shows up on his Instagram; his girlfriend, Tina, is Asian, and the Friday girl was infinitely not so. And I hung out with Kim and Adera and spent hours laughing. I did *not* post that I was at Max Cooper's house with a bunch of people because I didn't want Macy to interrogate me about his every move. So yes, I had fun. Unlike right now.

"Yeah, it was cool," I mutter, hating that I am making chit-chat with him. Thankfully, we are interrupted by Nate.

"Bro!"

"Bro!"

Right. Speaking "bro." An art form that I have yet to understand.

"We're gonna play *Fortnite*. You in?" Nate says in his regular voice. No character work involved when it comes to bro-speak.

I want to ask him where McDimple is, but there's no way I'm going to be obvious about having a crush on his cousin. Also: I hope Nate doesn't tell Macy about seeing Max Cooper in Fair Harbor so I don't have to endure twelve thousand questions about what Max Cooper said and who he was with and blah blah blah.

"Can't. I had to drop off some shit at the firehouse—gotta get back. Come through later, we're gonna be kicking it."

"Cool, cool."

It's a total body relief when they both ride off into their *Fortnite*-ian fantasy lives. Mostly because whatever Max Cooper wanted to tell me about Macy has been dropped.

*   *   *

Ravi Srinivasan, my shift relief for the summer, rides by on his bicycle, his surfboard under one arm, steering his bike with his free hand, McDimple and Nate behind him. This is practically the eightieth time I've seen Nate today, which is normal—there's only one town in Fair Harbor, one place to get everything you need. They park their bikes on the wooden bike racks across the pavement road in front of Crabby's and approach my counter. I can tell they've been at the beach: their hair is wet, towels are shoved in their metal bike baskets, and there's sand clinging to Nate's calves.

"Is it busy today?" Ravi asks, peering in to see if Sue's around, and when he realizes she's not, he grabs a few peppermint patties, so quick I don't have the chance to slap his hand away. He throws one to Nate and one to McDimple, then unwraps one and pops it into his mouth. Well. He's an employee, so Sue can deal with him.

Some words that aren't a sentence slip out of my mouth as I try to maintain eye contact with Ravi, but I can't help myself, I keep looking over at McDimple, distracted by how he takes his T-shirt off, using it to rub the perspiration off the back of his neck, and I wonder if his skin is soft.

"Wait, what?" Ravi asks, because, hello, I just spoke gibberish. I've known Ravi forever, like I have Nate and Macy. He has shaggy ebony hair, and he grew like ten feet over the winter—he's really tall now, and he's got the same problem I have, annoying zits that sit right under his bangs. Ravi has been coming to Fair Harbor every summer since he was a baby, and when we were twelve, we made out every day for a week, and I am pretty sure I'm the last girl he's ever kissed.

My personal repertoire of skills when it comes to sex is limited to open-mouth and closed-mouth kissing; I have sexual curiosity, obviously, but none of that applies to Ravi. Or Nate. Or any of the boys in our friend group, other than the new one, Leo McDimple.

"No, it's been so slow. I can tell you all about every customer I served today," I say, speaking to the air above Ravi's head and not at the dimple factory that I want to wrap my whole body around.

McDimple is now looking directly at my face, and his mouth curves upward, and his dimples, oh, his dimples appear! It's like we're Romeo and Juliet right now, and I wish we were, but with a happier ending than theirs.

"Are you guys going back to Birch?" I ask, hoping McDimple will say more words to me, but sadly, it is Nate who answers.

"Nah, everyone's scattered," Nate says, and then all the boys start talking in monosyllables. They walk into Woodson's without saying goodbye or anything else to me.

Ravi barrels into the shack—the way into Crabby's is through Woodson's, after all—stows his surfboard in the back, says hello to Sue, then plows his way into my zone, taking over my spot behind the counter.

He hip-bumps me—playful, of course; he's not a jerk.

"Get out of my way, sis."

"You're early, Ravs," I tell him.

"Ten minutes is not early, Jasmine Jacobson," Ravi responds, laughing.

I am a stickler for punctuality, but I'm also so anxious to meet up with Macy that I don't mind leaving work early. I doubt Sue will care. She favors Ravi anyway.

Marcelle Karp

I put my card in the antiquated punch-out clock and text Macy, letting her know I am on my way.

As I leave the shack and enter the comparatively cavernous Woodson's, I walk right into McDimple and Nate, who are standing in front of the counter where the pies are displayed.

"Where you going?" Nate asks.

"Macy's."

McDimple is looking at a pie intently. "You think our moms will want apple or blueberry?" He lifts both pies at me, as if I know the moms well enough to have an opinion. I feel like me and McDimple are officially on our way to becoming a couple (yes, I know, he is face-mashing with Alice Adams, but an average girl can dream).

"Our moms are twins. Sisters," Nate explains, as if I don't know that being twins also means being siblings.

Nate's mom, Sandy Beckerman, used to be friends with my mom, back when they'd piggyback our playdates with their day drinking when we were little. But I have no idea if Sandy Beckerman has a preference for apple or blueberry. "I . . . uh, go with apple."

"Thanks," McDimple says as he smiles, our eyes connecting, the world around me warping into slow motion, and all that there is now is the two of us until he breaks the spell with a question. "You coming to sunset tonight?"

The nightly ritual in Fair Harbor is to watch the sunset from the dock, as a community, which also means that my

24

friend group has a place to meet up, unless it's raining. So yes, I will be at sunset. I want to be around my friends and am still decompressing from a shitty year as a sophomore in a school that has way too many people. If I didn't have my camera and my carefully curated Jazzmatazz socials where I post my photos, I'd basically be lost in the wallpaper of my school like everyone else except for the one percent of popular kids. I don't have that feeling of being lost in Fair Harbor; I'm seen here, one of maybe ten people my age, and while every so often there's a new addition to the friend group, we don't have the kind of social hierarchy that exists at home.

Leo McDimple is a new part of this dynamic, and as Nate's cousin, he comes into our friend group preapproved.

"Yeah, totally. See you at sunset," I say. I'm poker-faced in my coolness, but I'm doing a Snoopy dance in my head.

• • •

Can you pick up two skirt steak strips from Saltaire Market? The ones I like, okay? I'll Venmo you now.

It's not unusual for Mom to text these requests, and I don't mind, since I've just spent the day in a shack listening to Sue breathe. Plus, these very specific skirt steak strips from the market in Saltaire are not carried in Woodson's, and they're delicious, so I run the Mom errand before heading to Macy's house.

> My Mom wants me to go to Saltaire and pick up steak. Come with?

Can't. Dealing with Olive. C u soon.

Bicycles are the primary mode of transportation on Fire Island. In general, the bikes here are beat-up cruisers. They get rusty easily, and every year someone loses one or gets one stolen on the big weekends like the Fourth of July, when a lot of day-tripping mainlanders visit. I've had the same bike since I was thirteen, and I love it; it's purple with a banana seat and it's super beat-up and no one but me wants it.

After picking up the steak, I ride toward Macy's block and see the gaggle of supermodels walking toward me, which is not a problem—lots of people walk and bike along Central Walk; it's the concrete street that runs through this part of Fire Island, separating the houses on the beach side from the houses on the bay side. The problem is that Leo McDimple is walking with them, and even though I'm riding by, I'm not speeding, I'm pedaling slow enough to see that he is walking really, really closely to the supermodel Alice Adams, like it's just the two of them, and they're a little separated from the pack, and he's looking down at his phone while she talks. And I picture them making out and I almost lose my balance as I pass by, and just as I yelp, he looks up and says, "Hey, Jasmine." I play it cool and yell "Hey" back, and I'm still within earshot when I hear Alice say, "Who's that?"

Exactly. Who is she to you, is what I want to know.

•   •   •

I turn on Macy's block, Birch, then get off my bike and park it in the bike rack that's in front of her house.

"Jacobson!" Macy yells from her porch and bounces off the steps to my side. She puts her arm around my neck and I wrap my arm around her waist as we walk up the stairs to her house, three steps leading up to it, white Christmas lights wrapped around the handrails.

Lilly Whelan, Macy's grandmother, comes out on the deck, her chunky red glasses covering her pale face—she doesn't go into the sun. She's a giant like Macy is, and she bends down to give me a hug. Lilly and Tom, Macy's grandfather, are super into everyone calling them by their first names. When I try to call Tom "Mr. Whelan," he always says, "That's what people called my dad." Har, har, har.

I adore Lilly Whelan. She just had her seventieth birthday, and me and Mom did a Jacobson tribute video for it, which she loved; she sent us a handwritten thank-you note. Lilly has a lot of energy, not in that tennis-playing kind of way, just in that way that she can do things herself and she gets super pissy if you treat her like she's fragile.

"Young flower!" she says to me, holding my cheeks in the palms of her hands and then releasing me. Lilly Whelan, in her big straw hat, her long legs jutting out of Bermuda shorts, walks down the stairs, waving at us. "Macy, honey, I need to go to Woodson's. You need anything?"

"No, Grandma, thanks," Macy says sweetly; I love their fan fest of each other, Lilly adoring of Macy, Macy in reverence of Lilly. I ask Lilly if I can put Mom's steak in the fridge, she "pshaws" me, meaning of course I can, and Macy and I head into the kitchen.

Macy takes the steak from me with one hand, holding my hand with the other, and she glances at the label. "You went to Saltaire? Why didn't you tell me? I would have gone with you."

"Um, hello, I did tell you?"

"Ah, right! Sorry. Olive-brain. D'oh!" "Olive-brain" means her mom was being a jerk; she's not a cool mom, she's an angry one, always on Macy's ass. "Did you see Max Cooper?" she asks, putting a slice of turkey into her mouth.

"No. I rode my bike, parked it, picked up the steak my mom ordered from the deli, paid, came here. Saw no one, spoke only to the deli guy and the people who took my money." I pause and, in this breath, decide I will not mention seeing him at Crabby's today. "Good that he was nice to you on the ferry, though."

"Yeah, it was good." Macy smiles. "I think he might like me again."

"Macy, you know he has a girlfriend, right?" That he cheats on. I pull up his Instagram, scroll through it, find one post, and show it to her. I'd rather prove to her that I'm right than let her wallow in a fantasyland where Max Cooper is open for business. "Look."

Macy takes the phone from my hand. "She could be anybody. He's just saying happy birthday."

Is she serious right now?

I take the phone back and confirm for myself that the photo I showed her has a caption that says, Tina Baby Love You Forever. Happy Birthday Girl. I scroll through more of his posts; this girl Tina is in a bunch of them, she's always sitting on his lap, and he's always looking at her like she's his favorite ice cream flavor. I think this girl means something that's more than "friend." Or she did.

Macy leads me to her room upstairs, and we settle onto her bed, lying side by side as Macy finger-combs my hair, inspecting the pink parts ahead of the upcoming task of re-applying the dye.

"Mace, do you know if that boy Leo is cuffed?" I ask, sensing Macy knows town tea, because she's been here since mid-May and I have not.

"Nate's cousin? Nah, I don't think so. Why? You like Leo?"

"I don't know him, Mace." I pause, wanting to know more, more, and more.

Macy starts giggling and tickles me. "You like him, you like him!" I wriggle away from her, laughing.

"I mean, today was the first time we've actually had a conversation. He came by Crabby's like twice." I pause. "But I saw him with that girl Alice Adams. Do you know her?"

"Yeah, she's staying a few houses down. I think they hang out. But, like, in a casual way." She laughs. "Tell him you want to take his portrait, and then you can hang out."

"I don't know. If he's hanging out with Alice Adams, what chance do I have?"

"What are you talking about? He'd be lucky if you gave him the time of day! You're way cooler than that girl." Macy stands up and lifts her lacrosse stick, swinging it overhead like she does when she plays. "You know, he used to come here when you were little. Before I even started coming here."

"Really? I don't remember him." I've been coming here since I was three. I'm tempted to text Mom and ask about this web of relationships, but that would cut into my Macy time. I have skirt steak strips in the fridge; I'll be seeing Mom soon enough. "You sure he used to come here?"

"I just *said* that. So, listen, what would you think about me painting this room black?"

I lie back on the bed, and we both stare at the ceiling fan, which is slowly distributing pollen into the ether.

"Paint it black? Your room?" Black? Isn't that for fashion and nail polish? I look at the chipped black polish on my own nails and think there's no way I could look at that color day after day.

"Yeah, what do you think?"

"Would your mom let you do that?" When I don't have a good answer, I reply to a question with another question.

Macy rolls her eyes. "Olive is so obsessed with her Tinder app, she won't even notice." I always love how Macy refers to her mom by her first name. My mom would never allow that; she likes her title as Chief in Command of My Life, aka Mom. "It would be cool if we both could paint our bedrooms black, don't you think?"

"There's no way. We're still renting our house here." My room in Fair Harbor is white, and I share it with Mom, and we share the house with her best friend Burt and whoever his girlfriend is, and his sister, Theresa. Renting with all of them makes Fair Harbor affordable for Mom, who's a New York City public school teacher. Mom only spends money "as needed," but getting out of the city in the summer falls under that umbrella, so we've always done it.

"Whatever." I toss a pillow at her and sit up, checking the time on my phone. "I have to go take photos of Adera. Wanna come and be my assistant?"

"Um, no." She laughs. "Adera and me aren't really gelling right now."

What does that mean? Of all of us, Adera is the newest to the friend group; she started coming to Fair Harbor when we were finishing eighth grade. I don't remember there ever being any weirdness between her and Macy. Everyone likes Adera.

"What happened?"

"Nothing. I mean, seriously, it was nothing." Macy bites her lip. "But you know. Go do your thing. And I'll see you at sunset, cool?"

Sunset. Where Leo McDimple will be. Hopefully without Alice Adams.

Cool. Cool. Cool.

• • •

"Did you work today? I came by with the kid, but only Ravi was there," Adera refers to the child she watches as "the kid," and most days, she stops by Crabby's to get the kid an ice cream cone. I honestly do not know this child's name yet.

We're shooting Adera's Instagram photos under the shade-friendly walkway to my house, which is surrounded by shrubbery, trees, and bamboo shoots. I'm standing on an apple box: I need the extra height; otherwise I'll get more under-chin than she'll like. Even though it's a perfect setting for a summer day—the sky Facebook blue and the clouds barely there—the sun would create stark shadows, so shooting here is better light-wise, plus much more comfortable temperature-wise.

"I left like ten minutes early. Can you turn your face a little to the left?" My camera loves Adera MacIntosh. No matter what exposure I use, her dark cocoa skin glows, her brown eyes twinkle, and her smile is contagious, even when she's got poppy seeds in her teeth. Adera is wearing a sunflower-yellow bikini top and an orange sarong; she, like me, does not walk around Fair Harbor in just her bikini—each of us with our separate issues about our bodies, I suppose. As I shoot, I tell Adera about Macy seeing Max Cooper. I actually really want to know what the "aren't really gelling" comment is about.

"I think Macy's mad at me." Adera bends forward, a signature move of hers on Instagram, allowing for an iconic cleavage shot.

Like Macy, Adera is tall—she's five foot eleven, which is the height she's been since she was in eighth grade, and like me, who is five foot even, she hasn't grown since. I don't see Adera much during the school year because she lives in Jersey and her parents don't come into the city much, plus they're a little helicopter-y about letting her take public transportation on her own. Which I guess is why they like Fire Island so much; parents are less neurotic about our agency here.

"But why?"

Adera tsks as she stands up and drapes her right arm over her natural hair, which is flowing upward like a queen's tiara.

"I don't know. We were at a party at Max's before you got here, and, I mean this is so dumb, but he put his arm around me. It was nothing—I think he was just trying to do that white-boy move of touching my hair—and Macy gave me this look." Adera pauses. "I mean. Cone of silence?"

"Yeah." Honestly, not conflicted about Adera confiding in me about Macy. This is not trash talk; this is concern about their friendship.

"When we were riding home, she iced me. And then she texted me to never do that again. And when I was like, do what again, she was all, you know what you did. And the only thing I could come up with is that Max was touching me. And she hasn't answered any of my texts since."

Adera and me aren't really gelling, Macy said.

"What should I do, Jazz?" Adera asks, when I don't respond right away.

"I think you should not stress about it. It's complicated with Max Cooper." Meaning: Macy still likes him. "I'm sure the next time you see her, it'll be cool." I look at the frames I shot. I think I got what she wants. Plus, we're both starting to perspire. I suggest going into my house to get something to drink, and Adera is into it.

Macy will get over Adera talking to Max Cooper. We are part of a friend group, after all.

• • •

We are sitting on my deck, on the lounge chairs, the bay water our view, each of us with iced tea at our side. Adera is waiting for me to upload the photos I took with my camera—a Canon Rebel—so I can AirDrop them to her.

"I met this guy in Kismet last night," Adera says while scrolling through Insta stories, more specifically, the Insta feed of this guy whose photo she shows me. "We hooked up."

"He's cute," I say of this guy, Lyndon, who is topless in every photo, and I am not mad at that: he has a fifteen-pack, if that's possible; he is fine, fine, fine.

"Yeah. I'm going to go meet him after this." She smiles. "He's friends with Nate and Leo. That's how I met him—we all went to Kismet last night. Where were you?"

"My mom made me go to the Pines with her to see her friend Monte." I pause, because I want to know more about McDimple. "You know Nate's cousin Leo, right?"

"Yeah, that boy is fine." She smiles. "And he's single, so you know . . ."

"But what about that girl Alice Adams? Remember they were hooking up at Max Cooper's party?" I ask her, trying desperately to get some concrete information.

"Remind me what she looks like?"

"Tall. Redheaded. Like a model."

"Nah." She sits up. "Wait. Let me pull up her Insta." Adera finds Alice Adams's Instagram and snaps her fingers. "Yeah, yeah, I know this girl. And no, they are definitely not together.

He was hooking up with this other girl in Kismet the other night. A girl that works with Lyndon. Let's say her name is Karen. Or Becky," she says and we start laughing. "I think he's just having fun."

I'm looking at Alice Adams's Insta too; every photo on there—and there's like thousands—is of her, as if it is a professional Insta or something. She has fifteen thousand followers; I don't know anyone with that many followers.

"Is she an influencer or something?"

Adera shrugs. "I don't know. But she is definitely feeling herself."

Fire Island is such a tiny ecosystem, and there are so few of us who are exactly our age, and Leo, with his dimples and his all-around impossible cool, is hooking up with every girl except me.

So maybe we are just two people who like cameras and are heading toward a friend zone.

Dammit.

* * *

At six thirty, Mom comes home from the power walk that she does most days in the late afternoons, when the sun is still up but not blazing; she walks for an hour on the beach, barefoot, of course, listening to podcasts.

In Fair Harbor, dinner is not just dinner with Mom. It's "family time." I usually only see her at dinner because I work all day (well, until three), and she mostly hibernates, and so she is, like, the role model for sloth-dom, which, I guess is what summer break is for: lounging.

"Macy came back today," I tell Mom as we stand over the outdoor grill on our deck. My mom can do three cooking things—boil pasta, grill steaks and burgers, and pour cereal—so we rotate those things every day that Burt is not around.

"Oh. Did she have fun with her father?" Mom looks at me and touches my hair gingerly—sometimes she does that, like she hasn't seen me in a year, when really, it's the opposite: she sees me every day and we share a bedroom. Mom is shorter than I am, if that's possible, and most of the time, I don't mind her. Except when she starts talking about all the bands she used to go see in the olden times, like the Pixies and the Smiths and anything else that started with a "The" in the '80s.

"Seriously, Mom? You know what her dad is like. He spent the whole two weeks trash-talking Olive."

Mom laughs as she turns off the grill and plates our steaks. I follow her to the picnic table on our deck, and we take our seats beside each other so we can watch our fellow Fair Harborians walk by in the sand as they make their way to and from town.

"And Olive? What's the latest on her?" Mom is in her usual uniform: long shorts and loose T-shirt, long black hair up in a ponytail, never any makeup in the summer. I don't think she needs makeup, but she'd disagree: she's addicted to her black eyeliner.

"Yes, *Mom*. I just told you . . ." And just like that, she's annoying, and despite the nuisance of worry, I can still snap at her.

"What? You told me nothing about Olive so far," Mom says, defensive. She takes a bite of steak, swallows, and then starts again with the fifty-five questions. "Gayle came with Macy to the island, right?"

"Yeah. Dylan too. Why?"

"I'm being nosy, that's why." Mom cracks a smile, and I know she's just being a concerned adult because it's her natural instinct to care about other people. "That girl needs someone looking out for her. Useless father, narcissistic mother. I mean, come on. I'm glad Gayle hasn't quit."

Mom is very opinionated about the way people her age do parenting, but I don't want to waste time trash-talking Olive; Mom may have some intel about McDimple, and so I change topics.

"Mom, when I was little, did I know a boy named Leo who is Nate's cousin?"

"Well. Nate's mother has a twin sister, Emily, and *she* has a son, Leo. When you were all, I don't know, maybe four? I was friends with them. I mean, I would go over at night or they'd come here for a cocktail. For a while, Emily was sort of my Adera."

"What does that mean?"

"A backup hang."

I bristle. I *hope* Adera doesn't think of herself as backup. She's my friend, period. Not best, and not a backup, but a friend-friend.

"Mom, Adera is not a sloppy second!"

"That's not what I meant. I mean, I usually just hung out with Burt, and when he wasn't around, I'd find other people to hang out with. Like Emily and Sandy. But then, I don't know. We went back to the city, and Emily kept blowing me off when I'd try to set up a playdate. I haven't seen her in years. We don't even follow one another on Instagram. I barely see Sandy, and we're both here on the island!" Mom takes a sip of her water. "So, yeah. Why do you ask?"

"Well, Leo is here this summer. I kind of almost hung out with him today."

"That's sweet! I should text Sandy and invite them over for drinks."

I don't know what to do with this random thought of my mother's. Having a bunch of moms over our house for cocktails is as interesting to me as being in Mr. Wheaton's Great Works of American Literature class: so, not. "Mom, what would you think if I told you I wanted to paint my room black?"

Mom puts her fork down and looks up into the sky, pretending to think really hard about it, and then she says, "I suppose I'd have to pull out all my Siouxsie and the Banshees records and hand them over to you."

"Wait, are you saying you were a goth, Mom?"

"Yes, child of mine. I was a goth when goth was invented—you know, in the dinosaur era." It's a running joke between us that Mom is so ancient. It helps that she has a sense of humor about it.

That's the thing about my mom: even when I have a really dumb idea, she finds the humor in it. Except, of course, when I'm being a big jerk, and then she's kind of really scary.

●　●　●

And at sunset, this is where we gather: the dock.

I'm in my purple-hoodie-and-black-leggings ensemble with a white T-shirt underneath in case I get warm because with global warming you just don't know what to expect with the weather in June. I park my bicycle at the bike rack across from Crabby's, then head toward the bay, where Macy is waiting for me on the dock with the rest of Fair Harbor.

I'm relieved that Macy (also wearing a hoodie and, even though it's in sixty-degrees territory, short-shorts) is already out here on the dock. It's always awkward for me to be the first one here. I hear Dylan's high-pitched voice, then spot him riding his bike in circles with a gaggle of other kids his age, screeching at that obnoxious decibel level of pre-tweens.

"Where is everyone?" Macy asks as I approach. She's leaning against the wooden rail with the bay behind her and the mean swans below, who hiss at nothing.

It's way past seven; our friends *should* be here. I shrug, searching with laser focus for Leo McDimple as the sun starts to fall into the ocean, the sky a swirl of orange sherbet.

"It's weird because Leo literally told me to be at sunset," I say. "Twice!"

"Well, his loss. You're looking foxy. I think you got a little sunburn on your cheeks, though," she says, tapping my nose with her finger. Macy pulls out her phone and without her telling me to pose, I know what to do: I smile as she selfies us. And then she texts our friend group in our ongoing group chat, which has been in activation ever since we all got cell phones, wya, attaching the selfie of us here at the dock without them.

Kim and Adera reply: Kismet.

Macy looks at me. "Why are they in Kismet?"

"Adera is hooking up with someone."

"Not Max, right?"

"What? No, Macy. She would never go for Max Cooper. I mean, she knows you used to hook up."

"Correction: we dated." Macy purses her lips. "So Adera has a guy?"

"Yeah, this guy Lyndon that Nate and Leo introduced her to."

Nate responds: Moms making us cook dinner for them. COOK! SMH.

Nate attaches a shot of his face covered in flour. Dammit. This means Leo won't be here either. Argh.

FML. Let's go for a ride later.

Ravi: Sue has me in prison. Come thru.

"What a way to welcome me back," Macy says with less enthusiasm, if that's even possible. "Let's do a lap," she suggests as she walks toward the end of the dock, in the opposite direction of Crabby's, and I follow her, disappointed McDimple has to do family time.

"Hey, Mace," this guy says to her, and we approach the very end of the dock, where this skinny, tall dude is standing, the bay water calm behind him. He has bright orange sunglasses on and a sleeve of tattoos on his left arm, an intricate design of lines and circles in black ink; he seems way older than we are. Who is this guy?

"Hey, Eddie," Macy says, with oodles of perk. She wraps her arms around his neck, and he puts his around her waist and then they kiss, on the mouth, right here on the dock, like they're the only people here.

Macy disentangles from him. "Yeah, I just got back today."

"Cool. So, later?"

"I'll text you," she says as she takes my hand, walking me away from him.

"Eddie?" I whisper in her ear, making sure not to look back at him. "Eddie? He looks like he's a hundred years old."

"For your information, he is only twenty-one."

That's not information, not enough to explain their mouth-melding just now. "Who is *Eddie*?"

"Some guy I hooked up with before I got sent to see Monster Daddy. I haven't mentioned him because he's not important. Listen, can we visit Ravi? It's awkward now," she says, referring to Eddie, and I get it, I get it, she doesn't want to be within spying distance of some guy she's hooking up with; he's not the one she likes.

"Copy that," I say, squeezing her hand, our arms intertwined as we march toward Crabby's, the best of all plan Bs: just hanging with Macy anywhere is enough.

* * *

"Let's go for a ride," Macy says, impatient with Ravi telling us about the mushy waves he surfed today, which are frustrating for a decent surfer, like Ravi is, since they're basically waves for beginners.

"Can you wait for a half hour? I'll be done closing up by then," Ravi asks, and it's clear he doesn't want us to leave him; he's over work.

"A half hour?" I ask. "To just stand here?" I'd rather be riding through this side of Fire Island. "Let's just meet up later."

"Snap us when you're done," Macy says sweetly, as she mounts her bike and rides away from me and Ravi. She has the advantage of being an athlete, and I have the advantage of being a couch potato, and in this case, she has the edge, because her superpower outdoes mine.

"Gotta go," I tell Ravi, getting on my bike and pedaling as fast as I can to catch up to Macy, who is waiting for me at the end of this street, Broadway, one of the few paved roads in Fair Harbor.

"Let's go to Saltaire," Macy tells me more than suggests, and I nod, as we do my favorite thing to do together: be on our bikes, away from everyone except each other.

Saltaire is the town next to Fair Harbor, and the main road has a different name than ours: Central Walk ends in Fair Harbor and becomes Saltaire's Lighthouse Road, the only road connecting our towns. We ride by the house with the used bikes for sale in front of it, and we ride by the church with the garage sale signs on the front lawn, and we ride by deer, who are everywhere, grazing in grass. The wood-slat streets are wider than ours and the houses are spread farther apart and they're bigger than in my town and the air is crisp and warm and I love summer, I love it so much, even the gnats that zoom into my mouth if I don't keep my lips zipped shut as I ride.

Macy turns off Lighthouse Road and takes a right onto some rando walk, riding toward the bay—if we turned left, we'd be heading toward the ocean—and we pedal faster now and we're riding side by side on these wider walks, not talking to each other, but occasionally smiling, and Macy takes a bike-riding selfie of us—she can juggle a bike ride and a selfie in all the ways that I can't, because she's an actual athlete who has co-ordination mastered. We're on autopilot; I don't have to ask her where we're going and she doesn't have to ask me if I want to go left or right, we just pedal, mostly because the options are limited: you either ride to the bay in the town you're in or you don't. There's no riding toward the ocean—Fire Island doesn't have a boardwalk along the ocean, connecting miles of beachfront, like you see in Coney Island or Miami Beach. In Fire Island, the ocean side is purely for beach-type activities, and the bayfronts have centralized hubs ("towns") for their communities to hang out in. Seventeen towns and no Starbucks in sight; that's just part of the magic of this place.

We make a left when we get to the end of the street, to-ward town, riding along Saltaire's boardwalk. The walks here have different names than in Fair Harbor, and even after all these years, I can't remember the names of any of them, other than the one Max Cooper lives on, and that's Pacific, and of course Broadway, which is where their town is, but I always know where I'm going because I have ridden down every walk or street in the towns of Kismet, Saltaire, Fair Harbor, Dunewood, and Lonelyville, every summer of my biking life. I simply cannot get lost.

There are only a few people out in town tonight, like these three private school girls that we know but don't really like all wearing tie-dyed hoodies, and they look at us but we don't acknowledge one another. We ride past the gazebo and turn into the main part of town in Saltaire onto Broadway, where the library is and the fire department and the market and the softball field and the air tire pumps, and we don't see anyone we know, so we keep pedaling until we get to the main road, Lighthouse Road, and Macy stops on the tree-lined board-walk, shrouded in shadows. I pull up beside her. And by now it's pretty dark out and I'm mostly tired, not just from riding bikes but from the whole exhausting day.

"Should we head back home?" Macy asks, meaning, back to Fair Harbor. It's a blue pill/red pill choice. The options are to go right and into Kismet, where we can ride around and maybe find Adera and Kim, or go left, toward Fair Harbor, where our houses and couches are.

I lean forward into my basket and tap my phone. I'm annoyed to see that there aren't any notifications of outreach from any of our friends on the screen, and my battery seems to be on five percent. "Yeah, let's go to my house and watch a movie."

She pushes off toward Fair Harbor and our couches, but surprises me when she cuts a right on Pacific, stopping at the very last house, Max Cooper's house. It's this gigantic glass building on the ocean that sprawls across three lots—they literally bought a bunch of houses and knocked them down to make one big one—and to enter you have to walk along a no-trespassing path. In this darkness, with the lights on inside, it looks like a Christmastime light extravaganza from down here.

I pedal after Macy, stopping when I'm at her side; she's looking at her phone. "Did Max Cooper tell you to pull up?" I ask, wondering what we're doing here in front of his house.

Macy turns to me, her expression pained.

"Are you okay, Mace?"

I guess he didn't tell her to. One of the many problems with having a one-sided crush is this: you can get ghosted even when you send a Snap.

"I'm good, Moo," she says quietly. Macy spins her bike back around so she's facing Lighthouse Road, and she pedals toward it. Whatever else she's thinking, she doesn't want to talk about it. I watch her long blond hair disappear into the darkness, and follow her like I always do.

It's a real pain in the neck to ride your bike when it's super dark in Fair Harbor, especially if you do not have headlights attached to your bike, like me. The boardwalks running across the island are wood-slatted, and there are barely any street lights. Even for a veteran, it is highly recommended to dismount your bike instead of riding it along the walks, so you don't collide with a darting deer and tumble into the juniper bushes. I've come close to mastering night riding by steering my bike with one hand, and having the flashlight app turned on my phone, which allows me to see where I am going and not end up tick chum.

It's all part of the thrill of being here with Macy.

• • •

The sky is black velvet, the stars are scattered, and the air is breezy and cool. We park our bikes in front of my house, locking them to the rack so they don't get stolen while we sleep, and Macy Snaps our bike-riding escapade to our friend group as we walk onto the front deck.

Kim Snaps back a selfie in front of the Pizza Shack in Kismet, and in the background are Nate and Ravi. I guess they texted with Ravi and we didn't, but they also didn't text us to pull up. I have a pang of feeling left out.

"So they're all in Kismet?" Macy asks, probably feeling what I'm feeling: hurt.

"Yeah, maybe we should have hit them up again."

"Nah, it's cool. It's better like this. Just us," Macy says.

I don't like that we were all scattered tonight. This is the first time where everyone was just doing their own thing, instead of meeting up at sunset, then following Macy to wherever she thinks we should go after: the beach or her house or some boat on some dock that we sneak onto.

"Hey, Mom, we're home," I announce as I slide the screen door open. Mom and Monte are on the couch, talking while Mom knits, because of course she can do both without dropping a stitch.

Mom looks up, sees Macy, bounds up the sunken living room steps, and holds Macy in her arms' tiny wingspan. "Honey, I'm so happy to see you," Mom gushes as she sits back down on the couch, resuming her knitting. "How was your trip to . . . where did your old man take you?"

Macy sits on the couch across from Mom, and Monte and I do the same.

"Ugh, nowhere? Just his dumb house in Connecticut—it was *torture*. At least he has a pool. I just wanted to be here with Jazz the whole time."

Being on the couch now with Macy like this?

This is how summer feels to me: whole.

Wednesday
in June

Chapter Two

I wake up at 6:35 a.m. and run my routine: hit the outdoor shower, where I also brush my teeth; then I get dressed, attempt to brush my hair, put my phone in my back pocket, grab my camera, notebook, and pen; then head down to the beach where I'll shoot *Galentines*, a summer project where my technical focus is perspective, but my thematic purpose is: a love letter to Fire Island.

I am doing a summer photography project for two reasons: 1) it will look good on my college application under "extra-curriculars" and 2) taking photos is a way to own my visual language and has been since seventh grade, when Mom let me use her pre-iPhone camera, a Canon Rebel. Now, when I'm shooting, I imagine that the Rebel is my Excalibur, an extension of myself that I alone wield with authority, the way Macy uses her lacrosse stick.

And I have some guidelines for myself: I have to do it before I start work. I can only shoot fifty frames. Not one more frame than fifty. It's a practice in precision, really, to test myself as a photographer. And the setup is consistent: the ocean as a backdrop with something going on in the foreground. I'm playing with perspective, and it's challenging because on some days, every frame is blurry. I'm learning as I click. I have the notebook to take notes on what I've done; I'd rather not use my phone because the sand is insidious.

This is how I spend my mornings, before I spend the day on my feet at Crabby's.

I hop down the wind-beaten stairs to the not-quite-white sand to take my daily shot on Holly Beach, where I have the option of using the shadows cast by the lifeguard chairs if I want to play with perspective *and* light. I like having the structure I have set up for myself, even down to the timer I set for seven twenty so I can get back home, download the frames, select my shot, post it, and get to Crabby's by eight o'clock.

I put my props—two sugar cones I swiped from Crabby's—in the sand and take a shot of them with my phone so I can add it to my Insta story (I get lots of applause emojis on my behind-the-scenes stories moments), then write down what the ocean looks like today—blue, calm, three fluffy white clouds—and get to work, crouched in photographer stance, which, to the untrained eye, may look like I am pooping.

"Hey, Jasmine."

I'm startled by the unexpected interruption of another person—male—and I yelp, "Eeek," and also, it's Leo McDimple. He's wearing jeans and a mustard-colored Champion hoodie, and his black hair billows in the breeze, covering his face a little, and I just want to move those tendrils away from his eyes so I have all access to them. My goodness, he is ethereal in his form even at this hour. Meanwhile, my face probably still has drool crusted into its crevices.

The yelp also causes me to lose my balance, and Leo, with his quick reflexes, catches me by my arm, easing my fall onto my butt, and he starts apologizing, knowing he's startled me. "Oh, wow, sorry, I didn't, I didn't know that . . ."

"It's okay. I'm just not used to anyone being out here with me at seven in the morning, except for joggers and people who walk their dogs." I make sure there's no sand in or on my camera, quietly freaking out that Leo is in front of my face. "And I know this is gendered, but, like, this is my only fear, other than sharks, of some man, you know . . ."

"Ah, wow, Jasmine, I wasn't thinking. Yeah, of course. You know, actually, I've been watching you shoot from our kitchen all week." He hesitates, biting his lip. That makes sense; I'm shooting on Holly Beach, and Nate lives on Holly, in the sprawling house that I am in front of. Hence the use of "our" kitchen. Also: he has been *watching me* from Nate's house.

"Wait, I just heard how that sounds. It actually started when I got up one morning to check the surf, and there you were with your props, and you know . . ." He takes a breath, puts his hands in a T formation as he sits right beside me, the crouching tiger. "Wait. Reset."

"So you've been stalking me?" I laugh, one hundred percent enjoying how goofy he's being right now.

"Stalking? What?" It takes him a minute, but he realizes I'm messing with him. "Okay, okay, okay. What's the cone doing in the sand? And, oh snap, is that a Canon Rebel? That's *vintage*."

Did Leo McDimple just call my camera "old"?

"Okay, so many questions, Leo!" Everything is happening so quickly. And my iPhone alarm pops off. I have forty minutes to get home, download my frames, choose one to upload to my Jazzmatazz Insta and then I have to go to Crabby's.

"Ack, I have to go." I stand, flustered, not sure if I got to fifty because, hello, Leo McDimple is a distraction—not just him asking questions but his body this close to me right now, so close I can smell his minty-fresh breath.

"But I just got here." He has no idea I am as surprised as he is that I am sticking to my schedule, it's just that I can't be late for Sue because then she'll glower at me all day, and that is an unpleasant way to spend eight hours in a shack. "I woke up. And I saw you on the beach. And I scared you. So, you know, winning." He laughs, and my heart cracks into sixteen heart-shaped pieces.

"Well, next time, come a half hour earlier." I am so impressed with my flirt game right now. I start walking, then spin around, walking backward so I can see him when I say goodbye. He has his phone out and is shooting me, which makes me uncomfortable; it's not in my nature to be in front of the lens. I was able to flirt my way through it the other day, but I don't feel cute or even up to casual posing. I lift my camera to my eye and take ten frames of Leo, although honestly, I'd take a hundred if I had the time, and then blow them all up to poster size and line my walls with his dimples.

Okay, maybe that's going too far.

He seems surprised that I'm rushing off, and he follows me, not saying anything, his hands in his front pockets. I bound up the stairs that lead me to Fifth Walk, the walk I live on, and he's right behind me. When I get to the top of the stairs, I stop to brush the sand off the heels of my feet and put my flip-flops on.

"So . . ." he says, his hands flapping around like my heart is.

"So . . ." I say back, because, like, what is he going to do now, start kissing me?

"Do you work every day? It seems like you do." He knows I work every day? Also, I don't. I want to know why he knows that it seems like I work every day. I want to know why he was randomly walking with Alice Adams on Monday. I want to ask him to kiss me forever. But instead of doing what I want to do, I do what I don't want to do: I play it cool. Casual. Keep myself from smiling too hard.

The smile stays on the inside.

"So far, I am scheduled to work all week, except Sundays." We're walking now toward my house on the bay side, and I'm walking faster than I usually do, because I can feel time slipping away.

"I like your toes," he says, nodding at my multicolored toenails—pink, yellow, sky blue—the pedicure Macy administered last night when she came over after sunset, another sunset when our friends were all doing their own thing, so we just rode around into Saltaire and stopped by Max Cooper's house to take selfies with the light of his house shining on our faces (a warm light in the moonlight is an excellent combination). "Works with the highlights." He points to my hair, but doesn't touch it.

My face breaks out into a smile. This boy is saying all these nice things, something that's on my Jazz Jacobson list of things to have happen in my life: a boy appreciating me. Number one on that list is: Have a Boyfriend, because I've not had one, not ever. And instead of showing my appreciation with a thank-you, I laugh so hard I snort, which makes him laugh too.

We've arrived at the gates of my Narnia—the doorway that leads into my summer house—and I am within breathing distance of Leo McDimple. We're facing each other, and he's so tall, I'd have to lift myself on my tiptoes to kiss him, that is if I were to make a first move, and I'm calculating all the different ways I could do so, and he interrupts me with actual words.

"Are you going to Crabby's right now? I'll walk with you if you are."

He wants to walk with me to work. He wants to spend more time with me. Is that because he wants to be with me or talk about *Galentines*? Are we flirting or are we photographer-bonding?

"I have almost fifteen minutes to upload my frames and post them to my Insta, so . . ." I know I sound like a precision queen, but really every minute matters before I start work, and even as I'm saying *No, don't walk me to work*, inside I'm begging myself to shut up, shut up, shut up.

"Oh, what's your Insta?" He pulls his phone out, the 'droid, goes to Instagram, and looks at me, waiting.

"A 'droid?" I ask.

"Photographer's choice of phone camera," he says proudly. From an owner of a Hasselblad, I will take that as gospel. He knows cameras. But, to his point, 'droids do take better photos than iPhones. I've just always had an iPhone, hadn't considered owning anything else. "So, wait, your Insta?"

"It's Jazzmatazz."

Now. Ever since we mostly met at Max Cooper's free, I've been reluctant to follow him, so I haven't even looked him up on Instagram, because what always happens with me is when I am crushing on someone they see me watching their story or accidentally liking a photo from 2015, which makes it apparent that I've been Insta-diving. So. I just . . . didn't. Even though I wanted to. But now, now we are going to be officially following each other, and I'll be able to figure out the Alice Adams piece of this. "It's set up for my photography."

"Jasmine, these photos are awesome," he says as he scrolls through, and I want to seriously bring him indoors and never let him out of my sight ever.

"Thanks. Hey, listen, I have to go," I fumble all over myself, so angry I have to actually do something other than stand here with him, listening to him compliment me.

"Okay, well, I guess, later, then?" He backs away and lifts his phone, and takes a shot or twenty of me waving back at him, and we both laugh and say goodbye again.

Now I am fifteen minutes behind my personal schedule, thanks to a set of dimples. I rush into my house and go through the routine: open my laptop, which is on the dining room table, pull out the memory card from the Canon Rebel, slide it into the laptop, download the photos onto my laptop, check my notes, pore over the shots, nervous, as I can never be certain I nailed it—can't get cocky—but today I did, I did, even with Leo McDimple making me nervous with his presence. I choose the one that shows a little crack—it has personality, it's not bland or perfect, just like me and Macy—on the base of the left cone half-buried in the sand, and the whole time I'm working, I am in a state of cotton-candied bliss, mirroring the tranquility of these sugar cones that represent me and Macy, standing at each other's sides, forever and ever.

It's So Good To Have You Around

#truefriends #Miley #galentines #photography
#jazzmatazz #summerproject

＊　　＊　　＊

As I'm walking to work, I realize: I did not even ask him about
the Hasselblad; that's how nervous he made me.

＊　　＊　　＊

I'm at work, and it's busy for a Wednesday. I haven't had a
second to text anyone about my alone time with McDimple
this morning, which means I'm stuck with obsessing about
our morning instead of analyzing it with the experts—Adera,
Kim, and Macy. Meanwhile, he's ridden by twice and waved
both times, so it is like we are best friends; he's hello-ing all
over the place.

"Hey, girl, hey," Adera says, her scalp in a purple head wrap,
the sun sweltering hot today, the kid holding her hand. I peek
over her shoulder, taking note of two customers behind her,
and Sue lurking behind me somewhere.

"Did you end up hooking up with . . ." I whisper-ask.

Adera puts a finger on her lips, mindful that anywhere you
are, there is always someone eavesdropping in Fair Harbor.
"I'm going to go to Kismet in a little bit, so . . ." Her "so"
means she's going to be meeting up with Lyndon, which also

means she's still seeing him. And because we're standing talking in front of the kid, I can't ask her if she's into him, more than she was on Monday, or anything like that.

Kids don't need to know the personal details of their baby-sitters' lives.

Behind me, Sue makes a noise of managerial disturbance, designed to get me back to work.

Adera clocks Sue's vibe and leaves me to tend to a gaggle of tweens, my least favorite of the customers because they're indecisive, which makes them frustrating to serve. Plus, they are obsessed with taking selfies; it's obnoxious.

I don't mind any of today's nonsense because I am replaying this morning, at my door, with Leo, the way he whispers my name, *Jasmine*, and the way he did not shy away from my gaze and the way his dimples appear just for me. Or so I'd like to imagine.

* * *

According to Sue, at some point, probably after Fourth of July, one of the cashiers at Woodson's will come work here in the shack, which means I won't have to work as much as I am now.

I'm thinking of Leo asking about how much I work as I casually observe the Woodson's cashiers, Lark and Felicity, staring at their phones. Sue never allows me to scroll through my feeds, so I'm slightly jealous that they can, even more so when they are interrupted by Leo and Nate, who put their items on Lark's counter. She puts her phone down, and I watch her take in Leo.

So I'm not the only one affected by how attractive he is.

"*Jazzy.*" Macy sneaks up behind me as I'm finally done for the day being inside Sue's Sweat Pit. "Look who I brought with me to do a little shopping." She points at Leo, with Kim Chang now standing beside him, putting her stuff on the counter.

Kim has been part of our friend group since fifth grade, and she's, thankfully, not as tall as the rest of our friends, although she is taller than I am—everyone is. I had my first kiss with Kim in sixth grade, when she taught me how to kiss in general. Kim lives in Ardsley, New York, with her dads, Matthieu and Scott, and her four younger brothers—I can never remember much about them, including their names, so I just assign them numbers, based on age order. At least I have that in my brain's file, the ages of her brothers (7, 8, 12, 13)—and they live on the ocean side of Fifth, and whenever Monte visits, he always wants Mom to invite Matthieu and Scott over.

"Hey," I say to everyone.

"Ciao, bella," Nate says in an Italian accent, his chest all red and raw. I'm guessing he didn't put sunscreen on, the fool. He pays the cashier, picks up his bag of groceries, and follows Macy as she leads us all outdoors, where we all stand for a few minutes, deciding what we're going to do next.

"Let's go sit in the gazebo in Saltaire," Macy suggests, and Kim is into it. So it's decided.

Macy walks over to the bike rack, pulling her bike out, and Kim does the same thing, so now I'm alone with Nate and Leo, and I'm hoping Nate will go get his bike too so that I can be all alone with Leo, and then run away for forever with him. Where to? I haven't gotten that far yet.

"So, I hear you don't remember my cousin Leo? You know you guys used to take baths together," Nate says, still with an exaggerated Italian accent.

I look to Macy, and she shrugs. So she must have told them when they were at the beach earlier, which she was nice enough to Snap me about. But spilling my tea, without my permission? Not cool, Macy, not cool.

Leo knocks Nate over, Nate stumbles into me, and Leo murmurs, not intending for me to hear, but I do anyway, "Shut up, dude."

"Wait." I realize I missed something here—these two have a whole history about me that I don't know. "We used to take baths together?" And immediately, I want to shut my mouth because my mouth asked the wrong question.

"Most girls remember when they take a bath with me," Leo says, smiling, and our eyes lock, and oh my God, I feel warm under my armpits and in my stomach, and my neck is doing that thing it does when I'm nervous: it's flushing. I can't even speak. "Anyway, your shots of the cones are epic."

"Really? You think?"

"Yeah. I like how—"

"Yo, Leo, I don't got all day, you feel me?" Nate bellows from one inch away from us.

Leo ignores him. "Let me text you some of the photos I took of you." Leo hands me his phone, expecting me to type in my number, but it's a 'droid and literally the equivalent of a rotary phone: nothing I know how to deal with.

I recite my phone number, and now he has it forevermore, to text me all the hearts and kisses I plan to dream about.

If he isn't taken, that is. I need to find out what's going on with him and Alice Adams.

"So, see you at sunset, cool? Maybe you'll remember tubby time by then." Nate laughs.

I want to ask Leo if he will even be at sunset, because he said the exact same thing two nights ago and didn't show up. And by the way, a naked Leo with a naked me and not one flash to an image of it in the files of my memory bank? I am an idiot. Is it normal for sixteen-year-olds to start forgetting huge moments of naked time?

Nate and Leo ride off toward the ocean, and I catch Leo glancing back at me. He smiles and I catch it, right in my chest. And I can't move, so I just watch them like a starstruck fan, glued to the pavement I stand on as they ride toward the surf.

"You seriously don't remember taking a bath with that nugget?" Kim asks, her long, black ponytail swaying with judgment at my memory lapse, snapping me back to the here and now.

"You remember anything from before yesterday?" I joke, and she laughs.

"Come on, girls, let's go for a ride," Macy suggests, and so that's what we do: we go for a ride.

To Saltaire.

* * *

We are sitting in the gazebo overlooking the bay in Saltaire, our bellies filling up with Swedish Fish that we bought at Saltaire Market. There are two lifeguards watching over the little kids and their minders in the shallow end, swimming with their arm floaties and shrieking. Farther out, older kids who don't need adult supervision are jumping off the one diving board that I know of on this side of the island, the one that rests in the middle of the deeper end of the bay.

When I was a kid, Mom would bring me and Macy here all the time, to jump off the diving board while she took little videos to share with her friends on her Finsta. Yes, my *mom* has a Finsta. Whatever. Two summers ago, I was about to do a dive, showing off for Macy and Adera and Kim, and this idiot boy pushed me aside, basically into the water, so that he could go before me. Macy was so angry she jumped in the water, swam over to him, and held his head down in the water until the lifeguard kicked her out. Macy was basically expelled forever from swimming in the Saltaire bay. But, really, this is Macy's code: looking out for your teammates. That dude crossed a line, and Macy stepped in.

Okay, and she almost drowned the guy, and we all yelled at her, so.

"So, wait, he just shows up at seven in the morning, randomly, without you telling him that's what you do every day?" Kim asks after I download Macy and Kim about my morning with Leo, all three of us looking at the tons of photos he took of me on the beach when I wasn't looking, and in front of my house when I was.

"Jazz, you are so hot!" Macy says, favoriting all the photos she likes, which ends up being almost all of them.

I do like these photos of me. My smile is relaxed, my pink and brown hair is the right amount of messy, and my skin's a reflection of summer itself. I look . . . pretty.

"Yeah, girl. *Hot.* You gotta post them," Kim adds.

"Okay, I will. But. What is going on with him and Alice Adams?" I need information.

"Listen, Moo, we can make Alice disappear like that," Macy says, snapping her fingers. We laugh, because that's ridiculous.

"No, seriously," I protest. "Is he in a relationship?"

"Okay, take it from me," Kim starts, adjusting her bikini top, her boobs spilling out the sides a little. "I was with him, what, Sunday night? In Kismet? He was hooking up with some other girl. Not Alice."

So Leo's hooking up with rando girls? Am I a rando? "So he's like every other guy out here? Hitting up girls?"

"No, Jazzy." Kim laughs. "It's summer, and we're all hot. It's fine." She stops for a minute when she sees how frustrated I am with this information. "Okay, look. Here are the facts about Leo Burke: One. He's not taken. Not by Alice. Not by anyone. Two. He showed up at seven in the morning to watch you take photos. Three. Who wakes up that early, except you? You hear me? The boy is here for it."

"Am I the 'it' in this scenario?" I ask.

"You are totally *it*. Now, baby, start liking these photos he's sent you, so you can begin the age-old ritual of obsessively texting each other," Kim adds.

"Make sure you heart a few of these so he sees you're liking them," Macy suggests, basically giving me a How to Catch a Boy 101 lesson.

"Can a heart on a text pop up on a 'droid?"

"Good point," Kim says. "Send an emoji. But not more than two. And then he'll be like, only those two?"

I'm taking her advice seriously. I think Kim should start a How to Get a Boy service; her advice is necessary information. She is the most experienced girl I know when it comes to keeping someone interested; she gets with boys and girls too, and they all fall for her undefinable magic.

"I think Leo has a thing for you, Jazzy," Macy adds. "Wouldn't it be great if me and Max went on a double date with you and Leo? We'd be the it couples of Fire Island."

"Yeah, you just gotta get rid of Max's girlfriend first, and then maybe that could happen," Kim says, guffawing like it's the funniest thing she's ever heard.

"Max doesn't have a girlfriend, Kimmy," Macy says defensively. "At least he did not act like he did on the ferry. Or at any of those frees I went to before I had to go to Monster Daddy."

"Uh, yeah, he does have a girlfriend. I don't know what happened on the ferry, but he is in a relationship." Kim is taking a stand here, and she is not backing down. Macy bites her lip.

"He was just super nice, okay?" Macy looks at her Instagram. "Yeah, Jazzy, you need to go for this guy, big-time." Changing the subject from Max Cooper, knowing Kim will dig her heels in—two alpha females disagreeing.

"Girl, I wouldn't mind getting into a bath with both of you right now," Kim says fanning herself with her hand, which makes us all laugh.

Two boys ride by on their bicycles, and we know them: Benga Swanson and Max Cooper's brother, Evan. I had a light crush on Benga last summer, but he was not interested in me at all, and after Macy told him that I liked him, Benga was nice enough to tell me to my face that nothing could happen between us since he was going to college (Wesleyan) in the fall and didn't want any loose ends. It didn't hurt my feelings that he wasn't into me, though. Plus, he referred to a potential relationship with me as a "loose end." No.

There has to be a decoder book for boy-speak somewhere.

"Evan!" Macy calls out, jumping to her feet and practically falling over the rail of the gazebo as she leans forward on it. Both boys look over and shout out, "Hey!" and ride their bikes up the ramp to where we're sitting.

"You know that gazebo is for Saltaire residents," Evan says, joking, in his baritone voice. Both of them are wearing red tank tops that say LIFEGUARD, so I guess that's what they're doing this summer.

Benga sits next to me and puts his arm around my shoulders. "Girl, how you been?"

After we had our "talk," I realized that Benga was just a flirty, friendly boy and I no longer needed to confuse that with interest. Now I can sit beside him without feeling anything other than the basic feelings of friendship.

Kim clucks her tongue. "So? Wesleyan? Is it all that?"

"Yeah, sis, it was all that." He laughs. "Good year. Dean's list. Y'all applying to Wesleyan?"

"This year we'll be doing the whole college tour thing. So maybe," Macy answers. "Evs, how was your freshman year?"

We all turn to look at Evan, who's leaning against the rail of the gazebo, his back to the bay, facing us, legs crossed at the ankles. Evan is doughy around his midriff, and the way his body is formed right now, he looks like he has moobs. He's mostly quiet, which, to the untrained eye, might come off as rude, but he's not; he just doesn't tend to start conversations.

"Go on, tell them, E," Benga urges, his booming voice gentle.

"Aren't you at Wash U?" Macy asks.

"Eh. I'm transferring." He takes a gulp of his water. "Now I'll be at Baruch." He looks away from us. And no one says much, our minds filling in the blanks. If he's going to Baruch, it means he's failed at Wash U and his parents are making him going to a local school instead of spending the big bucks for private.

"What happened, Evan?" Kim asks.

"I don't know, dude. I got there. I was okay. Then . . ." Evan shrugs. "Now I'm taking Zoloft, and my mom's got her Find My Phone tracking me, and, you know. Here." He looks sad as he speaks, the words molasses on his tongue.

Kim gets up and puts her arms around Evan. "I'm sorry, boo." He hugs her back and wipes his eyes.

"So, Evan, where's Max?" Macy asks, which surprises me. I mean, they're in the middle of telling us some heavy shit, and she goes there? To Max? Kim raises her eyebrows at me, and I know we're thinking the same thing: *Macy, come on.*

"Good question!" Benga says, but doesn't answer her. "So, Jazz, you still taking photos?"

"You don't follow my Instagram, Benga? I'm insulted!" I laugh, but actually I am insulted. I have 312 followers; you'd think one of them would be a friend. I mean, Leo follows me now, and as soon as I remember that, I pull out my phone, find his follow, LeothePhotographer, and follow him, but I don't have enough time to scour his feed and find out whether he's taken because Evan gets loud.

"Ahh, busted!" Evan points and laughs, interrupting my distraction. I lift my phone and tell Benga to smile. Then I capture us, plus Kim, in a selfie, which I immediately post to my Insta story. My impulse to share is part of my daily approach to growing my Instagram following.

"Aight, ladies, it's been great catching up, but we gotta roll." Benga stands up and fake-curtsies, and then they're off again.

"Let's go to my house," Macy says as soon as they're out of earshot.

And so we mount our bikes and start riding.

* * *

As we're riding toward Fair Harbor, I get a text from Mom. I lean over my handlebars and read it while pedaling, which I do *not* recommend; this is a move one masters over years.

> I need you to go to Saltaire Market. Can you bring back their prepared salmon?

Why can't she get on her bike and do these errands herself? I pull over to the side of the road, so I can text her back.

> MOM. I'm busy with my friends. What's wrong with the Woodson's salmon?

> They don't make it how I like it.

I realize as I look up to see where my friends are that I am on Pacific, and that Kim and Macy are sitting on their bikes in front of Max Cooper's house at the end of this walk. I didn't know we were planning a pit stop, and so I ride toward them, admiring how his house is as cool during the day as it is at night; with the light reflecting off the glass walls, they almost look like mirrors. "Hey, guys? What are we doing here?"

It's basically weird that all three of us are sitting on our bikes in front of Max Cooper's house.

"I just wanted to see if Max felt like hanging out," Macy explains excitedly.

"Well, I have to go back to Saltaire Market. My mom wants me to pick something up for her."

Macy, who is texting, doesn't tear her eyes from her phone. Kim looks at Macy then at me.

"I don't feel like riding back into that town, is that okay?" Kim whines more than says. I get it. She's probably tired from lying on her towel on Birch. I get how taxing getting a tan is. "Can we just wait for you at Macy's?"

Macy tosses her phone into her basket and smiles, although

it seems a little forced, and her vibe is a lot more toned down now. "So, yeah, we'll see you at my house?"

"Sure," I say, annoyed that Mom is so lazy. Really, she is the empress of the Jacobson queendom, and I am her lowly gofer.

"Okay, Jazzy. But if you see Max Cooper, text me right away. We'll come to you," Macy says. I nod and push off from them, on my way back to Saltaire Market.

Riding through the towns is far less fun when I'm doing it without Macy. We like to explore as we go, ride down walks we don't normally see and look at houses, but when I'm alone, I just keep it simple, head to the center of Saltaire, park, pick up what Mom wants, return. And because I am in a rush—my friends are hanging out without me during my free time—I just do what I'm supposed to do: purchase salmon. I don't make eye contact with anyone, I don't see anyone I know, just a lot of kids riding their bikes and people playing softball in the Saltaire field and stuff like that.

The whole thing takes twenty minutes. I turn on Macy's block, and the high-pitched giggles of girls hits me as I approach her house.

Alice Adams and her friends are on the same narrow wood-slatted path that I'm on. Two of the girls walk by wearing bikini tops and shorts and flip-flops. I now know that Sekiya is the one with the thick black-and-crimson braids, and the girl she's walking with has a light blue baseball cap on, and neither acknowledges me as they maneuver their way around my bike, as if I'm completely in their way.

There's not enough room for me to walk my bike and pass everyone—can't they walk single file?—without falling off the boardwalk and into the shrubbery, so I give up trying to walk my bike to Macy's house and just straddle it, my ass not even on the seat. I really dread falling into tick-land, so I wait for the parade of pretty to pass me by.

Another girl with blond braids and brown aviators is taking selfies as she walks by me, so she gets a pass from addressing me—she's busy, I get it, these paths are scenic, the sky so blue, the shrubbery above creates an archway affect and is ideal to be shot in, or take shots of.

And then the worst thing happens: McDimple is walking toward me, his head down as he looks at his phone, Alice Adams in front of him, chattering.

All the giddy of my day takes a tumble.

And the most beautiful girl on Fire Island looks at me, her long beautiful red hair flowing, white frame sunglasses covering her face, a crocheted shmatte overlay, a bright fuchsia string bikini underneath, looking so effortlessly cool.

Today, I resemble a Teletubby exile, wearing every color they do, with my pale blue Crabby's T-shirt and denim miniskirt, my Lakers-purple Nikes, and pink highlights in my hair; not basic but also not someone you'd notice.

And just as I think she's going to say hello, I swear I see her leg in slo-mo, extending toward my bike, making me lose my balance.

I yelp, which gets Leo's attention, and he catches me, his phone falling out of his hand and onto the walk. Alice's friends stop talking while McDimple holds my bike with one hand, his whole rippling arm around my waist.

"Jazz!" I hear Macy and Kim yell from the porch, where they've been waiting for me, but I can't hear anything else, because Leo's arm is around my *waist*! I inhale him, intoxication sweeping over me upon impact.

"Hey, you okay, Jasmine?" he asks, his breath on my face. I can almost taste the chocolate ice on his breath, we're that close, until the chiseled butter that is his arm releases me. We're standing, Kim and Macy at my side now too.

And then everyone starts yelling.

"What the fuck?" Alice yells at me, and her friends, all her friends, stop talking and start watching us.

"Al, seriously?" McDimple bites back at her—I guess "Al" is her nickname—and her face scrunches into a fake ugly cry, and as she turns away, she shoots me a janky death ray, then stomps to the end of Birch Walk, where her friends are, and crosses her arms around her chest.

"Did she just push you and *not* apologize?" Macy says angrily. She throws her hands up in the air and starts walking toward Alice and her friends, leaving me standing here with Kim and Leo.

"Jasmine?" Leo McDimple repeats my name as I slide in and out of catatonic ecstasy, a poppy field of Leo. "You good?"

I can hear Macy's voice, loud and insistent, but I can only hear the words that Leo McDimple is speaking to me.

"Yes, thanks, I'm okay, just cool, cool, cool," I murmur, checking to see that Mom's salmon is still in my basket, which, thankfully, it is.

"Leo, that's not right, what that chick did," Kim says, hands on her hips. "You better say something to her or I will," she adds with authority, as if they've known each other forever, when really, this is how Kim is: a badass.

"I know," Leo breathes as he runs a hand through his hair, looking at me. Looking at me, and not at Kim.

With my foot, I roll down the kickstand and dismount the bike. And then I bend down and pick up Leo's phone, which is lodged under my front tire. "My bike rescued your phone," I say as I hand it to him, and I am aware that the cheesiness outweighs the act I just performed.

"Ah, Jasmine, thanks," he says as our fingers brush against each other. That he's hanging out with Alice is confusing; my friends told me they aren't together.

"You sure you're okay? I can help . . ."

"Let's go, Leo!" Alice Adams says, interrupting us.

"Jacobson, we're out!" Macy walks toward me, my white knight to the rescue, her voice snapping me back to the here and now. Macy will, on occasion, refer to me by my last name, and it always makes me laugh, and I'm good now. In one motion, she flips up the kickstand and starts walking toward her house with Kim following, leaving me alone with Leo.

"Okay, see you later at sunset, yeah?" Leo says, the second time today he's said that, so I'm basically going to consider it a confirmation of a non-date date.

I take a moment to enjoy almost falling into a tick pit before I take one step further, Leo and me running through imaginary fields of vanilla bean macarons in my mind.

● ● ●

Macy's put my bike into the worn-out wooden bike rack, but she didn't bring the salmon in, so I grab it and run up the stairs onto the deck and into the house, where I walk right into Macy's grandparents, who are playing Scrabble in the dining room, fishing rods hanging on the walls, some kind of actual jazz music playing throughout the house.

Kim and Macy are already upstairs, so I'm basically the center of attention right now.

"Oh, look who's here, my sweet Jasmine!" Lilly says when she sees me, in her bright green Pucci caftan, barefoot and relaxed.

"Hi, Lilly," I say, squeezing her.

"We just started our game; do you want to watch or do you want to spend your day riding around checking out the young bucks on the strip?" Tom says. He's wearing a faded yellow T-shirt that has a Grateful Dead logo on it, with bright orange swim trunks, his skin golden, his bald head slightly sunburnt, Clark Kent glasses on the tip of his nose. If he were any other adult, I'd roll my eyes, but it's Tom, and he's adorable.

"Now, listen, Jazzy, go put whatever you have in your hands in my fridge and come play a round of Scrabble," Lilly orders, before I have a chance to answer Tom.

And even though I would rather go upstairs and find out what Macy said to Alice Adams and also vent about what just happened, I do as I'm told. I put the salmon in the refrigerator, and then the rest of the day drifts away from me as I turn tiles into words and points.

And, by the way, it takes a half hour before Macy and Kim even come downstairs to check on me. Like what were they doing upstairs?

"Grandma, have you hypnotized Jazz?" Macy asks as she walks down the stairs, Kim right behind her, a waft of weed smoke trailing behind them.

"Yes. You can join us, or you can watch. Those are your options," Lilly says. "She's staying right where she is. Gayle has taken young Dylan to Ocean Beach with some of his cronies, so we have all day to focus on high scores in the quiet of my home."

That fun fact of Dylan being preoccupied does not bode well for any window of escape for me.

"Okay, Grandma, we'll play, but if you kick my ass again, I am going to have to challenge you to a duel."

The Whelans are a competitive group of sports fanatics, and that extends to Scrabble.

Kim sits beside me, and Macy joins Tom. Lilly plays solo, always, and it's easy to forget everything when your best friend's grandma is trash-talking your Scrabble moves. We're all patient with Lilly Whelan in ways that we aren't with our own moms. I'm not sure what spell Lilly casts, but whatever it is, we play until Mom texts, wondering where her salmon is.

WYA? It's time for dinner.

It's really the best get-out-of-jail card I could possibly find.

"I have to fold, my friends," I announce, showing Mom's text.

"Ah, well, do tell Ava we miss her, and we'd love for her to join us for a game sometime," Lilly says, putting a hand on mine. "Now scram. I'm in a groove!"

Lilly has been staring at her tile rack for an infinity; I raise my eyebrows at Kim, and she rubs my shoulder, ending with a squeeze, code for *help*, I think.

Macy mouths *love you*, as I get out of the Whelan household as quickly as possible.

Without forgetting the salmon, of course.

* * *

The sky erupts as I start riding home, in fantastical grays and whites, lightning bolts shooting above and every thunder rumble forcing my shoulders to hunch. I pedal home, careful not to skid or I will wipe out, the torrential downpour offering a little hydroplaning, the water is that thick on the wood slats. One of these days I should count how many revolutions it takes to pedal from Macy's house to mine.

But more important, I'm shattered, not from being drenched, but from knowing that there will be no sunset hang tonight, no non-date with Leo, no riding bikes in the dark with Macy. The rain rules the outdoors out.

* * *

I go to the fridge to get a Coke, and it's completely stocked, which means that Burt and his girlfriend, Miho, and probably Theresa have arrived, because when it's just me and Mom, the only thing in the fridge is Coke and bottled water—Mom doesn't drink alcohol or beer, and she only eats prepared food and, of course, her usual cooking staples. When Burt is here, we are guaranteed to eat well; Burt is a chef at a soul food restaurant in the West Village, and even his grilled cheese sandwiches are epic in that way that you're like, *How is that so yummy?*

And my always question after I eat a Burt meal: *Why can't Mom make anything this tasty?*

With the housemates here, it will mean an hour of my life of *So, are you keeping up with your blog?* (yes, and by the way, it's not a blog, it's an Insta, it's called Jazzmatazz, I post on it daily, only photos, no, not a lot of editorial, no, it's not a school project, it's for me) and *Do you have a boyfriend yet?* (no) and *What do you think of the new season of* Doctor Who? (confusing and awesome as always), and I don't mind talking to them, I would just always rather do it not-now.

But I guess the rain means I won't be going anywhere tonight, so enduring their questions will just have to happen.

•   •   •

"Can you explain why I had to go to Saltaire if you knew Burt was coming?" I ask Mom, who is lying in her bed, her iPad on her lap. I'm not sure if she is watching something or reading something; she's kind of zoned out.

"I'd forgotten." She puts her iPad on the nightstand between our beds. "So. Your day? A success?"

"In terms of . . . ?"

"In general?"

I bite my lip. My day has been a roller coaster—Leo surprising me on the beach is the highlight, and Leo rescuing me when Alice Adams's leg attacked my bike is another bright spot, but I don't want to get into the details of it right now; any boy talk with a mom results in hours of cringe-worthy mom questions. And any mention of Alice's knee jerk will bring out the Mama Bear in Mom, which is not a good look. "I don't know. Sue needs to wear deodorant, you know what I mean?"

Mom laughs so hard she snorts.

"Ladies, dinner is served!" Burt calls from downstairs.

Well, here goes an hour of answering questions.

At least there's a delicious meal involved.

•   •   •

It stops raining around ten, and we, as a "family," have finished watching an old-timey black-and-white movie, *All About Eve*, which is Mom's favorite. Burt suggests that he and Mom go for a nightcap, but what that really means is that he wants to go to El Muelle and hang out with its chef, Tony, and get drunk. Mom and Miho are down to go, but Theresa is tired, and she goes to sleep.

For me, this means I get some time to myself on the couch. Burt tends to stays out very late, drinking brown liquor until Mom and Miho schlep him home. Luckily, there's no driving involved, just a lot of stumbling and cursing.

I text Macy: WYA?

She doesn't answer, at all, as I sit on the couch, laptop on my knees, working on Jazzmatazz, fans whirring above me, iced tea beside me.

> What did you say to Alice Adams?

> Told her to step off. More tomorrow xoxo

If Macy is telling me we'll talk tomorrow, she is probably with a boy—maybe that sleaze bucket Eddie. I send a group text to my friends: LMK if anyone is having a house hang.

No one answers. Maybe everyone's gone to sleep early? That happens sometimes. Even here in Fair Harbor.

I post one of the shots Leo took of me. I'm laughing, and my brown hair does not look like mud, the pink highlights are dancing in the wind, and he has somehow managed to make me look tan, and my hoodie is a little off my shoulder, and the photos Leo takes of me are the only ones in my entire life where I can look at myself and not hate what I see.

My phone buzzes, a text from Ravi. Dammit. My drama-free night is interrupted by a *boy*.

> Come out on your deck yo.

I get up off the couch and go to the floor-to-ceiling screen doors of our house—at night, you can't really see what's on the deck from inside the house—so I press my face against the loose mesh screen and see Adera facing the moonlight taking selfies, plus Ravi sitting beside Nate on the steps of our damp deck, smoking cigarettes, and finally, Leo, crouched in the sand, facing my house, shooting my friends.

Leo taking photos of Adera and Ravi and Nate.

"What are you guys doing out here?" I ask, trying to be casual, while inside I'm doing somersaults. Leo McDimple is on my deck, at my house. I slide the screen door open and then shut it behind me. It's hotter out on the deck than inside my house, which is unusual for Fire Island, where the temperature usually drops to the sixties at night. The boys are in T-shirts and shorts, except for Ravi, who isn't wearing a shirt, which, hello, brave—the mosquitos are out too, and I slap my exposed neck, manna for them.

"This one wanted to come here," Adera says, pointing at Leo. Adera is exquisite in a simple tank dress, white against her dark skin, formfitting, accentuating her curves.

"I was telling Leo about the view from your top deck, but he doesn't remember it, so we figured we'd come check it out," Ravi says. When we were all in elementary and middle school, Mom would have parents come over with their kids, and the parents would go to the upper deck and drink and smoke while the kids stayed here on the lower deck, playing in the sand and running in and out of the house, letting bugs in.

"See, I don't remember bath time and you don't remember the deck, so we're even," I say to Leo.

"I don't think so, babe. I seriously do not think you can compare a view of a sky with a view of me . . ." Leo stops talking, spins around, his fist closed at his mouth.

Did he just call me "babe"?

Everyone starts laughing and poking fun at Leo for calling me "babe." And he gives everyone except me the middle finger, and we laugh even harder while Ravi meanders down the steps of my deck to the bay and starts splashing about.

"Where's Macy?" I ask as I sit beside Adera on one of the chaise lounges.

"I don't know," Adera answers, moving her legs, making room for my butt. "She didn't open my Snaps."

So it's not just me. Macy's blown off Adera too.

"Yeah, this whole roll just kind of happened," Ravi explains as he comes back onto the deck and sits on the floor opposite me and Adera. "These guys were at my house and Adera came over . . ." That's typical here; everything is so casual. It's so much better just showing up at someone's house than waiting to be Snapped.

"What happened to the boy?" I ask Adera.

She tsks. "Girl, he blew me off."

I scowl. I was so excited for Adera to be in like with someone who liked her back.

"And may I remind you, he"—she points to Leo, speaking in a low tone—"wanted to come *here*." And then she whispers, "No mention of Alice, at all."

I nod, absorbing the information. Cautious in my urge to be enthusiastic.

"So, can I see this famously epic view?" Leo asks, the air thick with things flying across our eyes. I swat at whatever it is that lands on my forehead.

"Yeah, sure, let's go up—maybe you'll remember it," I say generically to everyone, even though I really want to be inviting only Leo upstairs.

"Can we smoke up there?" Nate asks in a Russian accent, which of all the accents he takes on is the best I've heard so far.

"No, dummy. My mom will lose her mind if she catches us."

Nate tsks and says something about how I'll never stop being a Goody Two-shoes. I don't take my preference for following the rules as an insult.

Ravi says, "Yeah, cool. You bring Leo upstairs. We're gonna take the boat out and smoke a bowl."

Adera nods her head, indicating that I need to take advantage of this moment; yes, I can interpret that much from a mere chin cocked at a certain angle, eyes wide open, nose doing a twitch.

Leo looks at me. "I'm game if you are."

I nod, because of course I am game. "Ravi, you know where the pump is for the boat and . . ."

"Dude, this isn't my first time here. We got it." Ravi steps off the deck and heads to the space that's between my house and the house next door, where we keep all the inflatable boats and pumps (we share them with our neighbors). Ravi tells

Nate and Adera to come help, and while they're getting all pumped, I hand Leo some bug spray.

"It's intense up there," I tell him.

He laughs. When he's done mosquito-proofing, I take him in through my house to the staircase that leads to the upper decks. There's a telescope up here and the three "walls" have settees with cushions, so I plop down on one, and Leo just walks the perimeter of the deck, bouncing in glee and looking out over into the bay.

"Jasmine, this is amazing," he says in a low voice. I'm staring at his back, and the shirt is pulled up a little so I can see some of his smooth skin. I feel a tingle and wonder what it would be like to have my fingertips on the exposed spot, how soft it would feel. Leo stands up and spins around again, taking in the view of the harbor, and then he sits down beside me and pulls out his camera.

Holy shit.

It's a Leica.

No one my age has a Leica *and* a Hasselblad. These are very, very fancy cameras.

"Do you mind if I take some photos of you? The light is perfect."

"Is that a Leica M10?" I ask, knowing it is. I have never ever seen one in person, or seen a person I actually know holding one.

"Yep. You're not the only person with a cool camera," Leo says, laughing, this secret he's known about himself all along, and only now, allowing me to know too.

He has a Leica and a Hassleblad. What other fancy cameras does he own?

"You know, those photos you took of me earlier are like the best photos ever taken of me in the history of the world."

"Yeah, I dabble too." Leo stands on the bench so he's hovering above me, snapping away, and I'm watching him, and maybe he feels my lustful coveting-his-camera stare and then he points his Leica at me and I hate being photographed—I have an awkward smile, and my face looks like an eggplant. "I, um. Hey," and other indistinguishable sounds come out of me.

"Don't tell me you're shy." He moves away a piece of hair that's fallen on my face, my dumb eggplant face, his fingers brushing my skin. "I want to see more of you," he says, and it sounds creepy, but it's not creepy the way he says it, and his eyes kind of close and then he opens them again and I wonder what he's thinking.

So I break the tension because it's just weird right now. "I'm more of a behind-the-scenes girl." I laugh and show him how terrible a subject I am, stretching my arms out in front of me and then lying back on the settee like a drama queen, and my motions are exaggerated, and he laughs; he gets that I'm a terrible model, and then I realize my boobs are swishing and swaying and when I'm lying down they're just a massive blob, so I roll on my side, my cheek pressed into the crusty softness of the cushion. Leo jumps off the settee and crouches in front of me, and I'm staring at Leo's beautiful face, well, with the slight obstruction of the Leica, and he tells me to keep looking at him and how great the moonlight looks on my skin.

"Just do you, Jasmine," he repeats, spoken like a real photographer, buttering up the subject so you can get the best shot.

"Dude." I pause and prop myself up on my elbow, and my sweaty boobs swish downward to my side too, like sloping wet tube socks. "I have to tell you something really important."

Leo puts the camera down next to him and looks right at me, and if I weren't so obsessed with his camera, I'd reach over and pull his face on top of mine. "I want your Leica."

And we both burst into giggles.

•   •   •

The mosquitos and the other flying creatures prove to be too formidable even for my lame attempt at flirting on the deck, so Leo and I go back into the house and fall into the couch in the sunken living room. I ask if he wants iced tea, and he does, so I get him a glass and sit across from him, my back to the bay, and he's facing the bay but looking at the photos he took.

"I don't even know which one I'm going to put on my Insta. They're all great," he says, and then he stands and walks over to where I'm sitting and plops down next to me on the couch to show me his photos. I can smell him, salty and a little sweaty too, and his breath is steady and relaxed; he is so comfortable in his body, so easy in his movements. He shifts his legs, his body leaning into mine, and this sensation of our skin, even with my clothes on, it's everything: electric, excellent, and any other *E* that's awesome I can imagine.

"Look at this one, it's amazing," he says almost in a whisper, like it hurts to say the words.

Just as I'm about to comment, Nate ambles in, amped up.

"Freakin' Ravi went to meet up with Julian," he explains without us asking why he's completely interrupting our lovefest.

"Who is *Julian*?" I ask.

Nate looks at me, flustered as he sits on the other side of Leo. "I don't have time to explain Julian."

"And Adera?"

"She left too," Nate mutters, fully in regular Nate voice. He must be tired.

I look at my phone, and yep, there it is, a text from Adera.

> I hope you're hitting that sweet thing.
> I want a full update manana.

This is the beauty of female friendship. Your friends can be two steps ahead of you, acting in your interest. Adera left early so I could be alone with Leo. Or mostly alone.

Nate says Leo and Alice are not a thing.

I ask Nate if he wants an iced tea, and he makes a crack about having a beer, and I get him an iced tea and sit beside him while Leo goes to the bathroom. Adera's text burning in my brain, I want to ask Nate about what he told Adera, but Leo is bound to come back from the bathroom.

I have to sit on this information. And enjoy it. Props to Adera for extracting it from Nate.

Nate starts scrolling through the photos Leo took on his Leica, and I'm listening to the drunk people walking along the shore in front of our house and suddenly realize it's about one thirty in the morning and Mom and them are not home yet.

Why won't Nate take Adera's lead and leave?

"Dude, you are so freaking fire," Nate says to Leo as he walks back into the living room. "You made this dummy look hot." I throw a pillow at him. "You should post this on your fancy photo Insta, Jazz."

Nate follows Jazzmatazz; he is, after all, an artist. Last summer, he let me take his portrait here at the beach, and I love that series of him lying on his surfboard, cropped from his waist up, some with his eyes shut, some with his N95 mask on. They're all in black-and-white, and his crystal green eyes are almost ghostlike, the way they blend against his very tanned skin with all the color drained out, he reminded me of the Night King from *Game of Thrones*.

"Maybe I will, if you don't mind, Leo," I say, wishing Leo were sitting next to me instead of Nate.

"Dude, check out Leo's website. It will blow your snap-happy mind!" Nate says. "He's a freaking legend already!"

"Do we really want to sit here and look at our phones?" I ask, not wanting to share Leo time with my screen. It's one thing when I'm with my friends and we're just scrolling through our feeds; it's another thing to do it sitting next to Leo, when I could be talking to him.

"Look at how many followers this loser has," Nate brags, showing me Leo's Instagram profile, and wait. What? He has a bajillion followers. 189,605 to be exact. How did I not notice when I followed him earlier?

"Come on, bro." He is almost bashful, meeting my eyes and then looking away and then back at me as I take Nate's phone from his grubby, overstaying-his-welcome hands.

Nate is rambling on in the background; I can't hear a word because my eyes have blocked out the world. All I hear is what is in front of me on Leo's feed: me.

The first photo on the feed is of me, from my first night out, and all of us were standing in a line practically on the edge of the dock, looking at the purple-streaked sky at sunset. Everyone is blurred; the only person in focus is me, fixing my ponytail, so my arms are up, elbows out, and I'm just looking ahead at nothing, clearly not noticing Leo, and my belly is a little exposed, my hoodie is flared, and my boobs are in a spectacular position, full and high, what with the way my arms are flexing. I'm the only person facing the camera, and the caption says: Jazz hands. 81k likes.

Seeing myself through his lens sends flurries through my brain, a sugar high of admiration and awe of him, his talent, and his focus, his focus on me. I want to give him a thousand thumbs-up emojis, but I also want to be cool, but I'm not cool, and this, this is so major.

"Leo, this work, it's . . ."

"Dude, my cousin here is legit."

I stand up. Whoa. Whoa. Whoa. No longer cool, now completely and totally about to be very uncool as the realization that I've been in the presence of someone who is as talented as the women I aspire to be, like Autumn de Wilde and Denisse Benitez-Myrick and all these women I follow on Instagram, some famous, some not, all of them supreme behind the lens.

"You okay, dude?" Nate asks me, seeing the revelation eclipse me.

I point at Leo and start laughing. It's nervous laughter that makes no sense to them, but to me, it's my outpouring of embarrassment, how pompous I've been about my project when all along I've been talking to someone who is already doing what I plan to be doing. He's a known entity; my aspiration. I want to tell him how intimidated I am right now, that I'm sitting with a real photographer, and it's not just the amount of followers he has, it's his actual photographs, this gorgeous, brilliant parade of people and places and colors that I only get a glimpse of, and I almost want him to leave so I can look at every single photo and fawn without an audience.

"So, this morning, you listened to me ramble about—"

"Nah, Jasmine, you're like—"

"Jazz, don't listen to my fool cousin. Google him. Leo Burke. Dude, tell her about your awards and—"

"Stop, Nate. Come on." Leo is blushing and annoyed that his cousin "outed" his talent. I get it; I get uncomfortable like that when Mom is praising my photos or whatever.

Still, it's like, *Leo, please, you have the gift of seeing the world, let us bask in it.*

The sliding screen door creaks, which gets all of our attention, and I turn to see Burt, drunk and unable to focus, flanked by Mom and Miho. Mom, seeing Leo and Nate here, looks very relieved.

"Boys, can you give us a hand?"

●　●　●

Later, after everyone's left and Mom is snoring, I am lying in bed, unable to fall asleep, going over the day, this insane day, of Macy staring at her phone and of Leo on my deck and of Adera's intel and of me on his feed. The thoughts swirling, one into the next. I can't keep up with any of them.

Leo is not cuffed.

I send a group text to my girls: I just spent the night with Leo. Not in THAT WAY. So much to tell you. Look at his Insta and let's discuss.

So I dive into Leo's Instagram.

I want to see everything, read every caption, see who follows him, who he follows. I want to know as much as I can about his craft but also him.

He has 1,672 photos posted, and I am scrolling to the beginning of the feed, working my way to the recent photos, and his Insta is filled with abstract photos of shapes and shots of landscapes and scenes of nature in motion, and then there are the people, the people he captures without them even noticing the camera, people moving through their lives; oh, his talent is boundless, boundless in its beauty and in his empathetic visual voice.

Several series on masks: masks strewn, people wearing masks, a rainbow of them. He has many portraits of his mother, and Sandy Beckerman, her twin, and a lot of them together. Oh, and there are a ton of photos of Nate sleeping, not just here in Fair Harbor, but other places, I guess places they've been to and some from Nate's brownstone on the Upper West Side. Leo seems to find Nate sleeping on every surface in Nate's house—Nate with his face smushed into a pillow, Nate with his mouth open while he sleeps, Nate being Nate even in his dream state, a basic goof.

My phone freezes, and I have to restart it. I go downstairs to get a snack while I wait, a bowl of chocolate pudding that Burt whipped up, and bring it back upstairs with me to swallow quietly while I scroll through Leo's feed. My phone is up and running, and I pull up Leo's Insta, not remembering where I left off at, so I start with the most recent post, which is of me.

Of *me*. Leo's posted another photo of me, eight minutes ago, from the batch of photos he took of me tonight, upstairs. I look ethereal. My face consumes the frame, it's practically black-and-white, but that's the beauty of this shot, the lack of color is an illusion; my face is pale in the moonlight, my brown eyes look almost green, and he's color-corrected the settee cushion to look midnight blue, and my lips are wet, like I'm wearing lip gloss (it must be the perspiration), and if this weren't me, I'd think, *Oh, this girl is not so bad-looking.* His caption: Moonlight Jazz. 423 likes.

I forward it to Macy, who is probably asleep; she hasn't answered any of my texts.

Are you awake?

That I am featured on Leo's Instagram? It's a big deal. Other than his family, he doesn't put people from his personal life on Insta.

There's one more photo of me, which means his three most recent posts on his feed star yours truly. And this one, the first one of me (so basically, it's a Jazz series) that he posted on Monday. I am behind the counter, leaning on it, my arms propping up my chin. I'm wearing a purple tank top, and my black bikini top straps are poking out at the base of my neck, my dark and pink hair in a high ponytail just like Ari, and I can feel the boredom seeping through my screen—he's managed to bottle it up in this one shot. This girl—me—is every girl you've ever seen, and yet she's not wallpaper: she's a Jedi warrior mixed with Ariana Grande. The caption reads: The girl at Crabby's. Jasmine. She was my first kiss. My first bathtub buddy. My first girlfriend. 105k likes.

MY FIRST GIRLFRIEND?

WTF, LEO BURKE?

I forward this one to Macy and to Adera and Kim too. These will require group analysis. I have all this conflicting data on him: he makes out with girls, but he spends the night with me. I've seen him with Alice, but then he shows up to my morning shoot. And now this, my appearance on his Instagram, with these captions that are a part of our shared history, one that is nonexistent in my memory.

Is this just content for his feed? Is something possibly happening between me and Leo? Or is he just a really good caption writer? Which is not my favorite of the options.

She was my first kiss. My first bathtub buddy. My first girlfriend.

The Next Day
Thursday
Still June

Chapter Three

I wake to a blinding gray light, the remnants of the rainstorm still looming, and a poem metronome-ing *My First Kiss. My First Bathtub Buddy. My First Girlfriend* in my head. I am sleep-deprived. I got what, maybe four hours? These are the mornings where having this routine is not welcome. Still. I have to get to *Galentines*; those shots won't happen without me.

And also: maybe Leo will be at Holly Beach too, with a Hasselblad or a Leica, shooting me at work. Telling me he likes my toenail colors or something.

I take my outdoor shower, the water in the open air waking my body up. Weighing everything of last night, Adera's texts, and Leo showing up and those captions about us as children. I put on my purple swirl bikini with my denim skirt, grab my gear and two brown Barbies, then head to Holly Beach.

On my way I text Adera, Macy, and Kim:

ALL HANDS ON DECK. COME BY
CRABBY'S AND I'LL TAKE A BREAK.
NEED TO DISCUSS LEO.

I bounce down the stairs and jump onto the sand. The beach is empty except for three strawberry blond Labradors chasing one another, their owner standing at the shoreline, cigarette to his mouth, a baseball cap pulled low over his face.

But he's not Leo.

My First Kiss. My First Bathtub Buddy. My First Girlfriend.

I turn to peer into the Beckerman house, looking for signs of life, but I don't see any movement on the deck. No Leo at all.

Leo and Nate were at my house until two a.m. He's undoubtedly asleep. Like I would be if I weren't shooting *Galentines*. I look at my phone: 6:41. I'm early, even for me.

Focus, Jazz, focus.

It's hard to focus.

He's not here. I shut my eyes, hoping he'll be here when they open. But he's not.

Maybe we were just . . . hanging out, nothing more than that. Maybe he posted the pictures of me because he's a photographer, and he puts series of photos up instead of one-off posts. Maybe him being on the beach with me the other day was a fluke just like last night, an opportunity for photographers to shoot and share.

Focus, Jazz.

I look back at the ocean, how turbulent it is. I turn one more time toward the houses, to see if Leo is on his deck, if Leo is walking toward me, if Leo is sneaking up behind me, poised to whisper-shout "boo," but no, none of that is happening, the Beckerman house is dark and listless.

Focus, Jazz.

I roll my neck and turn back to the ocean and my props.

I am on all fours in the sand, moving the Barbies around. Ugh, I hate my props right now. I pull out my notebook and write down the weather conditions—windy, white, wild—the scene I am trying to create, the purpose of it, all of the things I will need to remember when I choose my shot.

Maybe that's why he isn't here. Watching a true rube take photos of . . .

"Hey!" He calls out to me, from a bit of a distance, running toward me from the direction of Ocean Beach, and I sit my butt on my heels, watching him, his hair billowing in the breeze, no shirt—Leo is TOPLESS, which I know I've seen before, but it's still a novelty to be this alone and close to it, all for me—and black running shorts, really, all he needs is a horse and he'd truly be Jon Snow right now.

And then he's here, right in front of me, close enough that I can smell the coffee on his breath.

He drinks coffee?

"Have you been . . . running?"

Everyone thinks it's easy to ask your crush what you actually want to know.

It's not. It's preferable, but it's hard for me to form the words, the ones that amount to, *Hey, what is going on between us?*

"Yep. I don't do it every day, but I got here early and you weren't out yet, so I went for a quick run." Leo crouches down and surveys the Barbies facing the ocean, wearing matching pink bikinis, one with her hair loose and the other with a ponytail. "I figured I'd protect you from the creepers while you work," he says as he looks up at me, me who is adoring him.

Leo is here to watch me *work*.

"Is that okay?"

He is referring to my photography as "work."

"Jasmine?"

I snap back to attention; his captions about me and his posts about me have dismantled my cool-girl game completely, and it was not great to begin with. I am lost in his face, this face, his flawless olive complexion, the way his dark eyebrows animate him, his eyelashes longer than mine, willing myself to be cool and not start rambling. "Yeah, sure" is all I am capable of.

"Okay, great." He falls onto the sand and puts his arms behind him to support his beautiful, very fit body as he leans back, watching me.

And I stop what I am doing. I want to work. But I want to ask him about his post. And about Alice Adams. Which is the more important thing I need to know, though? And how do I conduct a conversation that could possibly upset me (*Why, yes, Jasmine, I* am *in love with Alice Adams*) and still accomplish the work I am doing? Because whatever the outcome is, it will get in the way of my work.

"Leo," I start, my camera suddenly heavy on my neck, trying to hold back from rambling. I pull the strap off, freeing myself. "I wanted to actually talk to you about what happened with Alice Adams. On Birch."

Leo's jaw sets, and he bites his lip, and he sits up, his back straight; I bend forward, falling to my knees, a foot or so away from him, facing him as he looks out into the ocean.

"I'm sorry she did that to you," he begins. "I really wanted to talk to you about it when I was at your house last night, but I was nervous you'd be pissed. At me." He stops talking, as I fumble with the Barbies, my two Barbies that I want facing each other. He takes one and digs a little hole, and parks her butt into it. Like she's fitting into a little cup in the sand. I do the same thing with mine, creating a seat for my Barbie, and now, now they're facing each other. "That's better," he says, admiring our collaboration.

"Is she your girlfriend, Leo?" I channel my nerves into this work; the profiles of the Barbies will be the pièce de résistance of this shot, the way I envisioned, that way I designed it to be, and with the looming grayness of the cloudy sky hovering, the ocean behind the Barbies nearly black with a bit of whitewash swirls, it's going to be dramatic. I start to shoot my fifty frames, and I have to count them out loud so I don't lose track of what I am doing and so I don't make myself even more anxious waiting for his answer.

"Alice? No. No, Jasmine."

I look away from my camera, and at Leo, who is staring with deliberation at me, and I wonder if he's catching feelings for me the way I am for him.

"Are you hooking up with, uh, anyone . . ." I falter, unable to finish my sentence.

He laughs. "I guess Kim told you about the other night in Kismet?"

"Yeah." I am still holding my breath, almost channeling the forceful energy of Kim and Macy and Adera, my experts on boys.

I need to get a low angle on the dolls, so I lie on my belly in the sand.

"So, no. This will sound shitty, but that was a girl I made out with. Not a girlfriend." He stops. "Are you, are you seeing anyone?"

Did he just ask ME if I'm seeing anyone?

I drop my camera, and he lunges forward, catching it before it reaches the sand at the precise moment my timer goes off.

What. The. Hey?

"Shit, I have to get to work," I say, fumbling to get up, almost giddy about what I now know. Leo hangs my camera strap on his shoulder and leans forward, helping me stand. I want to lace my fingers in his and walk hand in hand with him, but he immediately releases me once I'm on my feet and we start walking to the stairs that lead to Fifth Walk.

I have so much new news in my head right now that I don't know if I can handle knowing about the meaning behind his posts. Maybe I'll ask him about those after I talk it through with my friends.

He puts my camera to his face and shoots ten, twenty, thirty frames of me as I back away from him, him advancing on me, the ocean playing its violin, waves crashing into the sand. And I'm covering my face some of the time, holding up the Barbies some of the time, and laughing the whole time, completely sad when he stops clicking at the bottom of the stairs.

"I am so into this camera, Jasmine." We wipe the sand off our feet and start walking toward my house, as if we've always done this.

"Me too. Now give it back. Also, you have a Leica and a Hasselblad."

"Yeah, but I don't have a Rebel."

We both laugh at the ridiculousness of him NOT having a Rebel when he has top-shelf cameras. And we're just standing here, and it's so easy being with him, in front of the entrance to my house, where I need to go through my frames and post to Jazzmatazz. If I stand for one more moment, I will be late to work, and I don't have time at all to unpack *My First Kiss. My First Bathtub Buddy. My First Girlfriend.*

I'm good with him not being cuffed.

· · ·

I upload today's post in the still of the house, the bay before me, the water a softer gray than the ocean water, the clouds starting to part ever so slightly with the blue poking through.

But none of that is as magical as the frames Leo shot of me.

Every shot Leo took is worthy of being on a magazine, a book cover, a website, a poster, a billboard in Times Square. He's never used my camera before, and instantly, he got the settings to his liking, my Rebel speaking his language while I'm still reciting my ABCs.

I AirDrop the photos he took to myself; they're all going on my Finsta at some point. But right now I need to focus on my fifty frames. Which are not a total disaster; I got the Barbies in profile the way I'd imagined them, and a warmth blankets me as I look at these frames: they're almost a sequel to yesterday's post. My two dolls, looking at each other, me and Macy, here for each other. She's going to like this post.

Well, when she finally wakes up and reads my forty-five WYA texts.

I'll Be There For You

#rembrandts #friendsisashow #galentines
#photography #jazzmatazz #summerproject

∙ ∙ ∙

The gray of this morning has burnt off, and the sun is out, the sky blue, cloudless, and it's hot in the shack. Last summer, it was hotter, though. Sue had the shields up, a barrier between us and the customers, defending us against droplets, which also turned the shack into a sauna. I left work every day drenched, my clothes a mess. But this season, the customers are at arm's length, leaning on the counter, which requires me to wipe it down every time a person does so, and it's intuitive, despite how much Sue reminds me.

It's only eleven in the morning, and I can tell already that more people are going to be in Fair Harbor this weekend than last weekend because a ton of people have been getting off the ferry at the last few arrivals. When that happens they stop at Crabby's to get an iced coffee or a snack before heading to their houses, even if they're schlepping their laptops and their screaming babies and their mainland ennui, where they've left their manners but managed to bring their privileged attitudes.

"I need three iced teas, no sugar, one iced coffee, no milk, no sugar, all large, right away," Alice Adams orders, her friends gathered around her.

How are people so comfortable in their bodies? They are in bikinis of the same style (string) and different colors, none of them are wearing anything else, although Alice Adams has a Gucci fanny pack resting on her narrow hips.

I don't have hips like Alice Adams does; my shape is classic hourglass: boobs, narrow waist, and hips.

"I got you," I answer, trying to minimize any bad energy. "Anything else?"

"Do you sell hot dogs?" Sekiya asks, her lip gloss sparkling.

I shake my head "no." Seriously: Hot dogs at eleven in the morning? That's gross.

"I like your lip gloss," I tell Sekiya, because I do, I like glitter in a lip gloss.

Sekiya smiles and says, "Fenty, shimmering pink." She pulls it out of her bikini top to show me—she stashes her lip gloss in her bikini top!—and she's so friendly! And then Alice Adams interrupts my bonding moment with Sekiya to tell me that they also want four grilled cheeses.

"Sue!" I call out to her as I prep Alice Adams's drink order. Sue works the grill most days, handling customers' orders for fried whatever, keeping it moving. It also means she can eavesdrop with ease. Not my favorite way to work with Sue; I like it better when she's in the back, dealing with her manager duties. Sometimes, she'll let Ravi handle the grill, but she prefers me to stay away from it. I think there's some sexism at play here, but whatever, it's one less thing for me to think about.

"Copy," Sue shouts.

"If you guys can move to the side, I'll take the next customer," I tell Alice Adams and Sekiya and the other two as I hand them their drinks. And lucky for me, they do exactly as I ask.

Macy and Dylan are right behind the Alice Adams posse, and it's a much better view already.

"Oh my God, I have so much to tell you," Macy says, adjusting her white crocheted bikini top, her belly firm and flat, the opposite of mine.

"I have so much to tell *you*." I'm almost gloating but keeping my voice low, because Alice is within earshot.

"Can I get a vanilla milkshake, Jazz?" Dylan asks, his hair wet and his body already tanned from being in the sun.

"No, Gayle told me to get you a grilled cheese sandwich, twerp," Macy says.

"Awww, Mace, come on. I won't tell."

"But I will." Macy winks at me. "Do you think I could get three grilled cheese sandwiches, well done, please?"

"Coming right up." I write out the ticket like I'm supposed to and put it on Sue's rack of food orders. "Three more grilled cheeses, please. They want them well done." Sue nods, her spatula pummeling away at the grill.

"Wanna go float in the bay when I'm done here?"

"Yes." Macy leans forward and touches my hair. "I think tonight we should do the touch-up, what do you say?"

I nod. Over the past week, the sun has been doing its thing, fading out my pink.

"Also, I saw his post. We have a lot to unpack." Macy winks at me and then looks at Alice.

"Jacobson, you have customers." Sue, ever on duty, interrupts us, seeing that I'm not in motion as a cashier and server. Macy laughs, and she and Dylan move to the side while I serve the people behind Macy. "The grilled cheeses will be ready in two minutes."

I don't mind. Better things await me. I have plans after work.

• • •

For my fifteen-minute break, all four of us are sitting at the edge of the dock, our feet dangling off the edge. Drinking milkshakes that I made for everyone, all of us looking at Leo's Insta feed, each on our own phone, analyzing *She was my first kiss. My first bathtub buddy. My first girlfriend.*

"He's so into you, Moo," Macy says excitedly. "Like seriously."

"Did you guys kiss?" Kim asks as she drinks from her vanilla milkshake.

"No, he didn't try. Maybe I'm too short?"

"Girl, no. The boy likes you," Adera says, and she too drinks from her milkshake, a chocolate one. "Here is my proof: He's posting about you, Jazz. Look at his Instagram. It's all just art shots. And then you pop up on there."

I process what Adera says about Leo as I look at the tops of our feet, suspended above the blue water of the bay. I pull out my phone and shoot our feet, post to my Instagram. The happiest of feet.

"He's too tall for me to make the first move."

All three of my friends look at me and start laughing.

"It's not a height issue, Moo," Macy says and Adera agrees.

I'm so relieved they're back to being normal-friendly now that Macy knows Adera's not into Max Cooper.

"Okay, okay, I get it, I am among the experts here, but . . ."

"Hold up. Experts?" Adera interrupts. "I'm an expert on . . . men? Ha, you flatter me."

"What's wrong with experts? You three know way more about boys than I do."

"Nice save, noob," Kim jokes. "So listen. He likes you. You need to press this." Kim can tell from my blank expression that I have no idea what she's talking about. "You need to be up front with him and ask him straight-up what is going on with these posts."

"I just want to ask each of you. Have you ever straight-up asked a boy you like whether he liked you?" Also, I have not seen Leo this morning. And usually by now, he's ridden by once.

"Well, Macy just basically stalks Max, so there's one strategy," Kim jokes.

"Awww, come on, Kim, I don't stalk him," Macy answers, and she's good-natured in her response.

"No, you just literally park your bike in front of his house every single day," Kim claps back.

"Wait, what?" I ask. I thought what we did was random. Is she really doing this Every Single Day? I get that she's not over him. But that, that is a lot. I look at Adera, who shrugs—she knows the impact of Macy's feelings for Max Cooper.

"Listen, are we here to talk about Leo or Max?" Macy asks.

My timer goes off. It's time for me to go back to work. I stand, while my friends continue to enjoy the sun on their shoulders and the breeze upon their soles.

"Let's take a selfie," I suggest, and our four heads become one as I click, click, click. I immediately upload it to my feed, caption: Because My Crew.

"Hit that boy up," Adera instructs, as I leave.

Like it is that easy.

* * *

By the time Ravi comes to work, I've made enough vanilla milkshakes to tap out our tubs of vanilla ice cream. I'm so hot, I feel the beads dripping down my back, my body covered in drench.

"Yo, chili, what's rolling?" Ravi says as he puts his apron on and a bandana around his head.

"It's like never-ending people today, Ravs. I've never seen it like this on a Thursday in June. Crazy."

"Yeah, bro. People getting their summer on." He looks to the back, where Sue is. "I hooked up with someone yesterday."

"No way." I high-five him.

"And I might like him? So." Ravi bites his lip, he seems a little nervous. Because he never like-likes anyone. I squeeze him, despite the possibility of underarm stank.

Sue ambles out of the back. "Listen, you two. Break this shit up and get to work."

We both look toward the counter, and it's a ghost town; no customers, for the first time all day. I'm not going to win if I argue, though, so I shrug.

"Hit me later, cool?" I tell Ravi.

I walk into Woodson's, and it's crowded, aisles filled with people picking things up, looking at labels, putting them back on shelves. They're here for the weekend, arriving to empty cupboards in their kitchens and rotting vegetables left in their refrigerators from the previous weekend. Weekenders are so basic. I hit the ice cream freezer and get myself a chocolate ice. I need a little pick-me-up.

Because Leo didn't visit. He didn't even ride by on his bicycle. Not once.

*   *   *

Macy and I are lying on our backs in the inflatable boat that Ravi and Nate did not deflate the other night, floating in the shallow bay water in front of my house, watching the ferry putter its way into the dock, other ferries on the horizon, on their way to Ocean Beach and Atlantique and Dunewood, towns farther east of us.

This is quite possibly my favorite place to hang out with Macy: on the water, in our inflatable boat, away from everyone, music playing on Macy's phone. Which is in a water-resistant plastic baggie. So the tunes are muffled, but whatever.

It's super sunny and hot, and Macy has taken off her top, wanting a seamless tan. She's a B-cup, and so when she takes her bra off, her boobs stay in place, not rolling over to her side or anything. I'm an all-over-the-place-cup, so if I take my top off, my boobs loll and flatten, turning my body into a blob of boob. It's very not-cute.

"What did you say to Alice Adams the other day, Mace?"

"I just told her not to mess with you." She laughs. "Basically, put my lacrosse captain hat on."

I laugh. "Okay, thanks, but I *can* stand up for myself, you know." I get why Macy did that, she has territorial leanings and is well versed in protecting her teammates. In this case, I am the teammate, and Alice is the opponent.

"Well, I'm sorry," Macy says. "But I know what I saw, and I didn't like it. So I let her know."

I love that she has my back, and I appreciate it, and now that I know what Macy said, I can drop it.

"So, I've been hitting up Max, and he's just not answering me," Macy says.

"So maybe don't hit him up, Mace," I turn onto my belly, my arms dangling off the boat into the water. The beauty of the bay water, other than how clear it is, is that there are no sharks here, so there's no chance of my hands being chopped off by one, ever.

"Ah, Jazzy, don't be mean. He's probably just busy," she says. She shows me her phone. "Look at how cute he is."

Macy shows me Max Cooper's Insta story. There he is hunched over his dumb acoustic guitar playing some Ed Sheeran–y song; it is a veritable siren call to her heart.

My inner cynic rolls her eyes at the sight of another white boy with an acoustic guitar. Meh. "What did you get up to last night?"

"Well, I rode over to Max Cooper's to see if we could hang, but he didn't answer my texts."

"Why do you keep doing that, Mace?"

"Don't you ever just walk by Leo's house to see if he's in there?"

"I mean, I shoot *Galentines* on Holly. Where he's staying. But no. I was doing that before I knew Leo was staying at the Beckermans'."

"Well, okay, this is sort of like that. I ride by Max's house to see if he wants to come down. If he doesn't answer my texts, I move on."

"But he has a girlfriend. So maybe he's not answering your texts because, hello, girlfriend?"

"Okay, fine," Macy says, brushing me off. "So, remember that guy Eddie? I hooked up with him. We ended up in Saltaire."

"Is Eddie a Saltaire person?"

"Nah. We just, like, had sex off Pacific," Macy says casually.

"In the sand? Wait, in front of Max Cooper's house?" I ask, surprised that she would want to have sex in the sand, because when she did it with Max Cooper last summer, she said it was really uncomfortable and that sand was everywhere. Why would she do that again?

"Technically, I guess." She pauses. "Oh, Jazzy, don't look so worried. I'm okay. I'm used to Max being thick. He'll realize soon that we're destined to be together."

I sit up straight in the boat, my boobs lurching up with me, a chill reverberating through my body, Macy's words one step too close to eerie.

*　　*　　*

Mom and I are sitting on the deck, watching ferries roll across the bay. We've just finished eating, and Burt and Miho and Theresa are on their way to the dock to watch the sunset while

I do the dishes and Mom scrolls through Leo's Instagram. Well, technically, we fill the dishwasher, and whatever doesn't fit into the dishwasher, we hand wash. It's a good division of labor considering Burt and Miho make dinner happen.

I'm not weirded out by Mom on Leo's Instagram, because she's very good at analysis; she teaches English literature, and she's become an actual expert at close readings—that is, understanding what an author is trying to say in text.

"So basically, Jazz, he's telling the story of the two of you. A *This Is Us* kind of thing."

It's a forever fuel, the way Mom puts it.

"But, Mom. I have no memory of us as a story."

"Well, that makes sense. You guys were like four, five. Ah, you were so cute, you'd walk along the beach hand in hand, speaking in gibberish. Actually, you were always holding hands, when you were in the house, or at the bay, or anywhere. I wish I'd had a smartphone then! I would have been Instagramming you all day."

Ugh, Mom.

Still, this is why I can talk to her about certain things: she has the memory, which means she has the stories I want to hear.

"Why didn't you tell me this when I asked you about Leo the other day?"

"You only asked if I knew his mom, silly. Oh, and you'd sit facing each other in the inflatable boat, your little legs stretched out and the soles of your feet touching. Burt would drag the boat up and down the shallow part of the bay while you two chattered. So cute! And by the way, here's something else: When Leo left that summer, he was inconsolable, and you know, they live in the city, Brooklyn maybe, and I'd text Emily once a week to set up a playdate and she kept blowing me off. And when I finally confronted her about it, she told me that seeing you would be traumatizing for Leo, and that was that. I never texted her again."

So Emily ghosted Mom? And that's why I never saw Leo as a kid? Now I understand how all those moments we had together faded away: they happened before I was seven, and I just don't remember much from before second grade.

"So, when he says something like, my first this and my first that, he is really tapping into a memory that's very special to him," Mom says, bequeathing me her philosophy of teen romance.

"But why does he remember it and I don't? I feel so stupid."

"Well, he's had the assistance of these photos to fill in the blanks, and I didn't take photos of you guys, not the way Emily did. Sometimes, a photo jolts a memory into a reality of your past. He must have just been looking at them for a while, so the memory's been more active."

Mom puts her phone down. I don't remember the last time Mom had a boyfriend, and I definitely do not have a memory of my own father, so I guess not remembering a boyfriend I had at four isn't that bad.

"Why don't we go to sunset, honey?"

"Mom, you at sunset? Come on." Even before the pandemic, Mom was not into socializing. Now she's even more of a hermit. "Sure. Let's go."

. . .

I lose sight of Mom the moment we get to the dock because she sees someone she knows, this lady that I recognize but whose name I don't remember, and they start walking toward the beach together.

But I do find Adera and Macy: they're standing at the edge of the dock, their backs to the world.

"Hey, guys," I say as I put my arm around Macy, and I notice all three of us are wearing white T-shirts. "Where's Kim?"

"Family movie night," Adera explains. "She's gonna come out later."

"No one's here. You guys wanna ride to Kismet?" Macy suggests.

"Yeah, but not into town, cool? I don't want to bump into that fool," Adera says, meaning Lyndon.

And since we don't have anything else to do and the guys aren't around, that's what we do. We ride toward Kismet, passing through Saltaire and not going into town, riding as far as we can, basically to Burma Road, which is the sandy road leading to the lighthouse. And we take a bunch of selfies and Snap at the crew and then Macy leads us back to Fair Harbor, the sky starting to turn to the blue velvet of nightfall.

And when we get to Max Cooper's block, Macy hangs a right in the direction of his house. Adera gives me a *WTF?* look, and I shrug. Macy stops at the foot of his house's path and looks up. She texts, then turns to us.

"Just seeing if he wants us to come through," Macy explains.

"I can tell you right now, Mace, he does not want us to come through." Macy rolls her eyes at Adera as Adera pulls out her phone and looks at her Instagram; I do the same thing, scrolling because what else is there to do?

I go straight to Leo's Instagram, and he's posted another photo of me—the sky behind me is illuminated pink, and we're at the dock, so clearly it's sunset, and the way the light hits my face makes me look like I'm ethereal, as if I am a character out of N. K. Jemisin, my brown eyes are actually gleaming, you can see flecks of green in them, my smile natural, my hair full, I'm basically a poster child for a summer of rainbows.

It's almost better than a text. Although of course, a text would be the best.

The caption reads: Listening to Jazz. 1k likes.

"Guys, Leo's posted another . . ." I start, but Adera cuts me off.

"Girl, he's obsessed with you!" Adera exclaims.

"Macy, look," I say, showing my phone to her, but she's zoned out, looking up at Max Cooper's house. "Macy?"

Reluctantly, she tears her attention from his house, directs it at my phone. "Oh cool." She nods, but she barely even means it, she's so distracted. She looks at her own phone and sighs; the text she's waiting for—from Max Cooper, I suppose—is not coming through.

And because it's getting dark, the mosquitos are beginning their feast on my flesh. After eight smacks on my neck and legs and arms, I say to Macy, "Okay. Let's get out of here. I'm a snack fest for the mozzies."

Adera agrees and pushes off.

Macy is the last to follow us back to Fair Harbor.

* * *

Macy and I are sitting in a misshapen circle on the dock with Ravi and Nate and Adera and Kim and Gus Stuto, and it's almost ten and we've just been talking trash and getting bitten by mosquitos and not wanting to go home.

Everything feels normal.

"Jazz, let's go for a ride," Macy whispers.

I don't want to ride away to anywhere; I'm waiting for Leo to come *here*. Since his last post, he's also posted a video to his Insta story of him waxing his surfboard, a snippet of Coltrane's "A Love Supreme" as the soundtrack. I'm using every effort of deductive reasoning to ascertain whether this is in homage to me or not; Leo does love his surfboard. But that is jazz he's playing, and not just any number—it's the master, playing his magnum opus about a Love Supreme.

Is his story about me?

Then why hasn't he come around today? Or tonight? Or DMed me? Or hit me up on Snap?

"Jazz!" Ravi half yells. He has this incredible talent of being sweet and annoying at the same time, but right now, he's more of a lifesaver, distracting Macy from dragging me into her Max Cooper rabbit hole. "Dude, you're way spacey."

"That's because there's no one upstairs," Idiot Gus says, pointing to his head. I guess he's saying I'm dumb. What a genius he is. I avoid being one-on-one with him because he finds a way to make fun of every single thing I say, but he's grandfathered into our friend group, he and Ravi and Nate are tight. I guess it's a version of bro loyalty.

"Very funny," I snarl.

"I wonder how many new birds will be here this weekend," Nate chimes in with a British accent à la Jason Statham. The "birds" Nate is referring to are the non-regulars renting in Fair Harbor, and really what he means is, will there be any girls for him to torment with his moony-eyed routine—you know the one, where a boy just stares at you and never says anything? Yeah, that's Nate's whole deal; he dreams about girls but is too intimidated by the female gender to speak to them.

"Well, you better get on it, Casanova," Macy says, "before you're off to France!"

"Wait, what?" I ask.

"Yeah, we're only out here for a few more weeks. Mum and Auntie Dearest are making us all go to Paris for the rest of the summer; they're working on an art project and blah blah blah. So I gotta get on the birds, mate. Stat."

Does that mean Leo is only here for a few more weeks too? I stifle what feels like a gasp and pretend it's a sneeze.

"Ha, maybe you'll finally kiss a girl," Ravi says, now that he's an authority on hooking up, not that anyone other than me knows that. "Someone that's not one of these two."

Macy gives Ravi a friendly shove. Macy is the only one of us who has made out with everyone, even this numnut Gus, and you couldn't pay me enough money to kiss his dumb face.

"Yo, Mace, we heard you smacked that chick Alice," Ravi says to Macy, and everyone, I mean, every single one of us snap our necks—that's how quickly we turn to look at Macy.

Also: What? When did that happen?

"I didn't *smack* anyone, stupid. Stop spreading rumors about me," Macy says. She stands and steps to Ravi, an intimidating sight, with long, toned legs, muscled arms, fists firm in a clench. It's clear to me she could kick Ravi's ass if she wanted. Clear to him too.

"Yeah, so what went down, then?" Ravi leans back in tone and also physically, away from Macy. Macy is practically a warrior; she could do some serious damage to any human being with her strength.

"All I did was tell her not to push Jazz into the bushes ever again. It was—as the British say—civilized," Macy says this so matter-of-factly it sounds normal.

Ravi looks at Macy, and his eyes narrow, everyone else is just watching them. "Okay, cool," he says, finally, but I can tell, just by the way "cool" slides out, he is really saying, *I don't believe you.*

"That's the smoke show Burke is with, right?" Gus throws out. "Shit, bro, that guy cleans up."

Gus has no idea the effect of what he's just said on me, even though Leo is not taken. That Alice Adams is considered a smoke show and I doubt I will ever be referred to in those terms is just triggering the insecurity I have about my general essence.

"And where is your pretty-boy cousin tonight, Nate?" Macy asks, knowing that I want to know this, but don't want the boys to know I want to know.

"Let me check his ankle bracelet," Nate says, and the bro-bros laugh at his dumb joke. Literally stonewalling us.

I turn away from my friends, rolling my eyes at Macy. She lifts her chin, basically offering me a way out of this awkward conversation I'm listening to.

And frankly, I'm ready to get some air.

"Well, I'm tired," I announce. I don't want to be hanging with my friends, I want to sit on my couch and find something to watch and not be sitting here waiting for Leo to show up.

"Wuss," Gus contributes, and I shoot him a death stare, which he ignores.

Macy reaches out, puts her hand on my arm. "Can I sleep over tonight?"

The answer is: YES.

* * *

As we go to the bike racks to get our bikes, Macy suggests, "Let's go for a ride first."

"I am legit tired, though."

I don't have the energy to explain I've been awake since six fifteen this morning, that I've been on my feet for a good part of the day, that I've been waiting for Leo my whole day, that the only thing I have the oomph for is my butt imprinting on my couch.

"I need the exercise, Jazz. Cardio does a body good!"

My heart does an eye roll as Macy rides away from me, and seriously, I did my cardio for the day when we went to Kismet. I catch up to her, pedaling double time; obviously Macy can outride me even in a sea of molasses.

"Dude, wait," I yell, and she laughs as she slows down and actually, I'm feeling better; the way the hot breeze slips through my hair is welcoming, almost like a second wind of energy plus glee, especially when we start riding side by side, singing, "One taught me love/One taught me patience/And one taught me pain," Ariana in our hearts, not really caring if we can be heard, knowing really that it doesn't matter, no one is going to stick their head out a window and tell us to shut up. We fly by the church on Lighthouse Road and take a right into Saltaire's town and ride by the softball field and the library and the market, and we get to the end of the road where the gazebo is, and there are people hanging out in there, but they're all old, like Mom's age old. We ride out to the end of the dock and stop at the very edge.

Macy inhales deeply, then pulls her phone out and takes a selfie of the two of us on the Saltaire dock and immediately posts it to her stories, my phone buzzing as she tags me.

"Should we do your hair when we get back to your house?" Macy asks as she texts, her fingers flying across her keyboard.

"Yeah sure. But let's also watch a movie or something." And I turn my bicycle around and start pedaling.

We ride by the library, and there on its colonial house steps stand Max Cooper and Benga, and I watch Max Cooper spot Macy and turn his body away, pretending he doesn't see her.

He is so lame. Ugh, I cannot stand Max Cooper. This isn't high school in between periods when there are so many people rushing to class you can't see in front of you. This is Saltaire, and there are maybe eight people out tonight in this town and two of them are standing on the steps.

Macy stops pedaling, and so do I, directly in front of Max Cooper and Benga.

We all "hey" each other.

"Max, I've been texting—"

"Yeah, yeah, chill, I've been busy." Max Cooper, as usual, making civility impossible for Macy.

"Literally just texted you."

I want to add, *Yes, I saw her text you, you dickwad.*

Benga nods at Max Cooper, who stands and says, "We gotta roll."

"Where you going?" Macy, ever hopeful, asks.

"Home," they answer at the same time and then look at each other and laugh.

"Can we join y'all?" Macy asks.

"Nah," Max says, and he kind of jogs toward his bike.

Benga hesitates, and then turns to Macy. "You know he has a girlfriend, right?" Benga doesn't wait for Macy to respond; he walks away from us, his head lowered, not making eye contact with me.

"You okay, Moo?" I ask Macy. I know Benga is not trying to be mean, he's just direct, but did he have to be *that* direct?

Macy blinks a few times, her lower lip puckering up and down; I put my arm around her, and her head falls into my neck, which slowly becomes wet from her face.

It takes us a few minutes to be on our way.

*　　*　　*

"Mom, we're home," I call out as we walk into the house, Macy flopping her body on the couch. I tell Macy I'm going to go check in with Mom, who is probably already asleep—it's way past her bedtime, but I haven't spoken to her since we had dinner earlier and it's frustrating because I have so much to tell her.

I head up to the bedroom and the lights are off and she is asleep; her strenuous day of lying around on the couches downstairs has obviously worn her out.

I come downstairs, my hands washed, and I sit beside Macy, who is on Max Cooper's Instagram feed. I get it; this is how we can figure out what boys are up to, putting these pieces of a disjointed puzzle together, their boy disease contagious as they post their mixed messages to us—we parse these out, following clues left on Insta or Snap. My whole generation will become new versions of Sherlock Holmes thanks to this training. But still. Looking at the little crumbs of clues Max Cooper left isn't going to make him like her any more than he does.

Max Cooper is not into Macy.

"Dude," I say, like in a warning kind of way. "Maybe you should stop looking at his socials."

Macy throws her head back in exasperation. "Why was he so mean?"

"Well, Max Cooper is a jerk, Macy. Can you work on getting over him? I mean, he has a girlfriend," I offer, meaning, *Get over Max Cooper already.* Plus, the asswad is a cheater.

"That's not helping, Jazzy."

I stop talking for a moment. Try to think. Macy still likes Max Cooper, I get it. But there are other boys out here, boys that, even though I find them *ew*, Macy has hooked up with. "What about that guy Eddie?"

"Eddie is a hookup. He does not compare to Max. None of them do," Macy says as she falls onto my lap, her body curling into a fetal position. I put my hand on her hair, stroking it, long laps down her thick blond mane.

"Macy, on a scale from over him to not over him at all, where do you land?"

"If I tell you, you have to swear not to tell a living soul," she whispers.

"Of course, I swear," I respond, a little louder than her whisper just now.

Macy sits up and our eyes are forever in each other's. "Not over him. At all." Macy laughs, and then she says somberly, "Listen, Jazz. Listen to me." She holds my hands. "You have no idea what love is, Jazzy. You haven't even had sex yet. Like what is that?"

"Aw, Macy, rub it in, why don't you," I joke, but I mean it too.

Also, and by the way? I dream about having sex all day long. Like obsessed with kissing someone, and someone kissing me and then doing all the other stuff. Okay, that sounds a little out there, but really. What I want is to love and be loved and to have sex and be sexed by the person that

I love and loves me back. I am the only person at school that still hasn't touched a boy in all the right ways. I mean, honestly. If I hear one more person tell me how to hold a penis by using a banana as an example, I will do something—I'm not sure what, but it won't be my best moment as a human being.

"I need you to be on my side, Jazzy," she says as she snuggles back onto my lap.

"I am on your side. You're my best friend, Macy."

"Then start acting like one. And start here with this as your homework: I need ideas on how I'm going to get Max Cooper back."

I swallow my voice because I know that there is no getting Max Cooper back. There is only one option for Macy: getting over Max Cooper.

The First
Friday in July

Chapter Four

Macy's body is warm against mine, and Mom is breathing deeply, although not full-fledged snoring, across from us. It's much earlier than my usual wake-up time; it's five thirty instead of my standard six thirty, and I feel frustratingly alone in this semi-light. I was up throughout the night, looking at my phone, waiting for a text, something, anything from Leo.

And nothing. Not a word from him. His Instagram has a TBT post—a shot of New York City, from April 2020, a barren valley of buildings without life really—but, like, it's not even Thursday anymore. Also: Why tell *me* to hit *you* up? Why not send me a Snap or a text or DM me?

I rub my face, this conundrum a sieve in my thinking.

The boy I like disappeared on me.

My best friend is not over this jerk of a boy.

This summer was becoming a bit brilliant, and in one day, it turned stunningly sour.

I fling my legs over the side of my bed, willing my body to roll with the momentum of it and get up. I take my shower outdoors, careful not to wet my hair because I let Macy touch up my pink highlights and I don't want the dye to run. I head down to the beach, the sky breaking even with the night, streaks of orange striping across the ocean in a state of calm save for waves lapping their way onto shore.

I am a full hour earlier than I usually am; being here on Holly Beach this early means I don't have to face my feelings about Leo not showing up. I didn't like the way I felt yesterday when I thought he was blowing me off on the beach and then all day, not hitting me up, and I don't want to feel it again. I can get ahead of disappointment if I just avoid certain traps, like waiting for him to show up, in person or in text.

I don't have any props with me today because I want a very, very simple shot: a silhouette. It will be of my hand, held out, the way I outlined it in my notebook. I want to see only blue behind it, maybe some clouds. I take a shot of my hand in the light—you can see the tiny veins under the skin of my palm—and post it to my Insta story like it's a test shot. I shoot my fifty frames, my hand held out, fingers splayed, the ocean glassy and peaceful, and because of the sheer complexity of holding the camera with one hand, and because of the angle, and because of the light at this time in the morning, the photos I take are eerie and epic and choosing the one to upload is in itself a challenge, because so many are great.

I Want To Hold Your Hand

#beatles #photography #jazzmatazz #summerproject

I really like today's post; it's a lowkey nod to Leo, of course, but it's also about Macy and me, how I just want to hold her hand and lead her away from Max Cooper.

• • •

My phone buzzes at 7:23 a.m. Instagram DM.

WYA?

Leo. He's looking for me. And looking at my Instagram. Finally. Finally some sign of thinking about me from McDimple. Despite my internal pep talk and my efforts to avoid waiting for him, it's still nice that he's at the beach, waiting for *me*.

I told you you gotta get up way earlier to catch me.

Playing it cool.

LOL.

And to that LOL, I say touché.

Marcelle Karp

• • •

Sue is working from home for a few hours, so Ravi is here with me at Crabby's this morning, making fun of every rude or indecisive customer (not to their face, of course—that would be mean). We're taking advantage of Sue not being here by having music on in the shack, something she never lets us do. Ravi's Spotify is on his playlist of Wu-Tang and Mac Miller and Anderson .Paak, and we're actually enjoying work, except for those hiccups where he starts rapping along, which is not a cute look.

It's mostly busy, especially for those fifteen minutes after the ferries arrive, filled with a lot of familiar faces from previous summers and a bunch of new ones, and it's encouraging to be recognized by the ones who have known me forever, to see me as an adult—well, almost adult—rather than some cute kid who gets her chubby cheeks pinched. I note every hot guy around my age that I haven't seen out here before as potential Macy options (only two so far, but it's still early in the summer. I mean, it's uncomfortable to be attracted to the older boys, like the twentysomething-year-olds, because they're just too old to like without it being *Lolita* weird, but still, the eyes cannot deny what they see), and I Snap the news to Macy, who is not opening any of my Snaps about the very attractive boys and how life behind the counter is the new Tinder.

138

"So, Jazz, I want to pick your brain . . ."

"About Macy?" I ask. He probably wants to unpack what happened with Alice Adams and Macy.

"Macy?" Ravi asks, confused.

"Excuse me, miss?" A customer interrupts us, standing by the cash register, needing whatever very important beverage he wants. And his loud twerp screaming at his older human, just bleating like a goat.

My gosh, I can't stand the sound of little kids.

And then right behind the harried customer stands Alice Adams. No friends. On her own? Weird. Since she's popped onto my radar, I've never seen her without her posse.

"Would you mind if Ravi helps me?" she asks as I'm about to ask her what she needs, and it's not a sweet request, it's a request of provocation. I don't mind rolling my eyes at her in front of her—this is beyond a customer/service person relationship; this cuts deeper, because it's two girls who like the same boy, and even with my little exposure to boys responding to me in any way, I know that can be messy.

"She sure doesn't like you, huh?" Ravi whispers.

I shrug as I head to the back to get another tub of mint chip ice cream. The tubs are the key to my goal of ripped arms, they're so heavy to carry, and also, lowering them carefully into the freezer requires precision control.

As I'm doing my weight-lifting medal work, I hear Alice Adams's voice call out, "Leo!"

I bolt up so quickly I almost bend and snap myself into a back brace. Leo is in the midst, and I am back, baby, back to some spark, knowing he's here, knowing I'll see him, hoping that maybe, just maybe, he's walking *to* Crabby's to see me, the same way he was on the beach looking for me. Sue shows up literally as I'm putting on lip gloss—wearing a denim dress that is right out of a prairie woman streaming series—and yells about how loud the music is and turns it off.

"Jeez, Jazz, I'd think you'd know better than to have this music on." She hands me a bottle of Mrs. Meyer's spray, indicating I need to clean or sanitize or quite possibly both.

As usual, I don't respond in any overt way. I keep my eye roll to the inside of my brain and head to the counter, and there he is by the bike racks across from Crabby's, Leo Burke, wearing a The Fall T-shirt and a purple Lakers baseball cap. He's got a Leica M10 around his neck, so clearly he's been out shooting.

"Leo Burke!" Alice says again as she abandons the counter, leaving her iced coffee behind. I'm standing next to Ravi, who is texting, and everything happening feels like it's in slow motion; she body slams Leo with a hug, this stunning, no-body-fat bikini-wearing girl, wraps her arms around his neck, and the imaginary conversations I've been running in my head with Leo come to a dead stop as I watch her meld into him.

Seeing them together, after not seeing him at all, and knowing that they're fresh out of a sort-of-together breakup?

It's stirring, and I'm the opposite of whatever I just was. I'm a scrap on the floor, flattened by a stiletto heel. That lump that's been sitting with me for the last day about him is back, jarred by what I can't unsee: the way Leo's body fits so well with Alice's. Maybe they're talking because they've kissed and made up and that's why he ghosted me yesterday and I'm back to being the girl in the shack, wearing a stained purple tank top that I've worn a million times and jean shorts that are not short-short hot and with a round belly.

Still, Leo isn't putting his arms around her; he tries to push her, gently of course, away from him, or at least that is what it looks like from where I'm standing.

I feel a heat within.

Ravi, who is dealing with another customer, pokes me. "Dude. Your customer?" Ravi motions at the needy blob standing in front of me, asking for an iced something or other. It's hard for me to hear him because all my ear-energy is trying to pick up what Alice is saying to Leo and what Leo is saying to Alice.

"Miss?"

"Yes, sir, I'm sorry. Iced coffee, no milk?"

It looks like Alice and Leo are fighting: her arms are folded across her chest; she's angry. "I did not . . ." she says, but I don't know what she didn't do—I have to leave to prepare a customer's iced coffee—and I feel a relief. They're arguing. They've not made up. Maybe he *is* here to see me.

I wrap up this transaction with my customer and retreat into the back of Crabby's and tell Sue I need to take my fifteen-minute break.

If Leo is still outside, and Alice is gone, I can ask him straight-up what is going on. Because if they are back on, yes, I will be, to put it mildly, bummed, but I can do what I always do when boys are not interested in me: get over it.

Easy to say, harder to do.

I make my way through Woodson's and bump into someone who says, "Excuse me?" and I mutter, "Sorry," and burst into the sunshine of Broadway, relieved to find Leo sitting on his bike, alone, possibly and hopefully waiting for me.

And I'm not sure what to do as I stand in the entrance of Woodson's for what feels like an infinity until Leo smiles at me, which is a green light to approach, and I do so as slowly as I can so that I can maintain my cool, trying to make sense of why he's still here, where the eff Alice went, and why his presence has such an effect on me.

"Jasmine, I like the way the pink is looking." Leo points at my head as I approach him, smiling so hard my teeth hurt, and I take in this pillow of joy before me, erasing the last few minutes of confusion.

And before I can say hi to Leo, Ravi runs out after me, but he's not interested in telling me anything—he wants to talk to Leo.

"Yo, that chick Alice was up my ass pumping me for intel about you."

Leo glances at me, and I can tell he is trying to see if I heard Ravi, and of course I did—I mean, he's practically shouting, and they're only a foot away from my body—and Leo says, "Yeah."

Sue screams out from the front, "Ravi, get your ass over here."

Ravi fist-bumps Leo and squeezes my shoulder before disappearing into the bowels of service.

"He's such a ding-dong," I say, the calm sweeping over me like a meditation app.

"That's one word for it. You done with work? I have some stuff I shot today I want to show you," Leo says, pointing at his Leica.

"Well, what I can do is give you ten minutes. That's how much time I have left on my break."

I start walking toward the bay, figuring we can sit on a bench and I can also inhale him as I find out what happened with Alice and he's just standing there and so I basically order him: "So, let's go."

"Where were you this morning?" he asks as he catches up to me, basically beating me to all my questions.

"Where were *you* all day yesterday?" I snap back, emboldened by my need to know if I should hang on or move on. I don't have a moment more of brain and heart energy to spare.

"Wait, what? I texted you. Like three times. You blew *me* off," he says, his hand brushing his hair out of his face, and it's like, *Leo, if I were just eight inches taller, I could have done that for you while also putting my lips against yours.*

"You sure? I didn't get anything from you." I stop. I don't want to get into an *I texted you; oh no you didn't* war. Messages get lost in the vortex. Clearly. "So, I have this question." I pause as he holds up his phone, showing me the texts he's sent: three WYAs and one Okay, guess I'll see you in the morning. I can feel my whole face go *ahhhhhh*. He *was* looking for me.

"I guess we should just DM, huh?" He laughs.

"Or get an iPhone like the rest of us," I murmur, which makes him laugh. We sit on a wooden bench on the dock, our thighs touching. Well, my bare thigh touching his blue jeans.

"Okay, so we're good?" Leo laughs as he puts his arm around the back of the bench, his fingers lightly grazing my shoulder, and it kills me, but because we are just facing forward, I have to pivot my body to face him, and I lose all physical contact with his body.

"No, I have more." I pause as I appreciate his dimples. "What was that about with Alice Adams?" I say it so quickly it comes out in one breath, one long word practically.

He blows air out of his face and opens his mouth to speak, closes it, and then says, "I told her yesterday I don't want to hook up anymore. And I know we weren't together, but I like being clear about things. I was always up front with her that we weren't exclusive, so . . ."

"So she was just yelling at you for fun?"

"I wouldn't call it yelling. More like, annoyed at the way I said hello, I guess," he jokes. "We are barely friends I think at this point. And do not forget this: I'm mad at her for pushing you off the boardwalk. That was so uncool. Not cool? Whatever, it isn't cool. And actually, I'm also pissed at Macy."

"Why? All Macy did was tell Alice not to push people off boardwalks."

"Uh, no. Yesterday, Macy showed up at Alice's house, and it was kind of weird. I had to tell her to step off."

"Wait, what?" Whatever it is or was, it's here, thick in the air between me and Leo.

We're interrupted by Ravi, who is running toward us, sitting on the dock. "Sue sent me, so don't shoot the messenger. She wants you in the shack, stat."

I look at my phone. I've been with Leo for way longer than my allowed fifteen minutes.

"Gotta go."

"But I haven't even had a chance to show you my stuff," Leo says, meaning it.

"Seriously, Burke?" Ravi laughs.

There goes what could have been the best fifteen-minute break of my lifetime.

* * *

I tell Sue I need to pee, and she rolls her eyes, wanting to know why I didn't pee on my lunch break, and I am skipping through her eye rolls because something is happening with me and Leo Burke.

But also: What did Macy do?

I go into Woodson's, and once inside the toilet space, instead of peeing, I FaceTime Macy, because this news is too huge to wait.

"Leo broke things off with Alice Adams, Macy! I asked him to his face and he told me to my face!!!!" And I whisper-scream it, because I am in a bathroom and the walls could have ears.

And Macy, who is on her bicycle, stops to the side of the road; I can't tell if she's in Saltaire or Fair Harbor, her beautiful face taking up the whole screen, and she raises her arms in the air, and the phone too, obviously, the sportsperson's sign of victory.

"Wow, wow, wow," her face, back in the frame, says.

"Right?" And then I pause. "But also, Mace, Leo told me you showed up at Alice Adams's house and it was kind of ugly? What did you do?"

"Nothing. It was silly. She needs more of a backbone." Macy is so matter-of-fact about it, it does sound like nothing.

Still, it's not enough. "Macy, but what did you actually say to her?"

"I told you, nothing much. Jazz, I'm your best friend. Who are you going to believe? Some guy or me?"

Someone knocks on the bathroom door. There's only one toilet, and I've been in here awhile.

"Always you," I whisper, always Macy, defeated that I'm stuck having to make a choice: my best friend or a boy I've known for less than a week. It should be an easy choice—Macy—but why would Leo make it up? He was there. He saw something I didn't.

"That's my girl. Okay, I'm heading to Birch right now. Come through."

I put my phone back in my pocket.

Always Macy.

• • •

Everyone (except Ravi and Adera, because they are working) is at the beach when I get there after work—Macy and Nate and Leo and Gus and Kim and this guy Paul Christiansen (he's cool; he used to come here when we were kids, and now he just shows up randomly, like right now).

"Look who's here," Macy announces as I rock up, and she hugs me, and she doesn't smell like vanilla—her breath is a combination of weed and beer, which, okay, school's out and all that. I look at everyone else sitting in the sand, in their swim trunks and bikinis, and everyone is drinking except for Leo, who's staring at his phone.

All my friends look up and say hello, and Leo takes a photo of me, from below, which means he will get more chin than actual face—well, from that angle, at least, and it's like, the first time all week when what we're all doing is what we've always done: our friend group just hanging out at Birch.

Macy puts her forehead to mine. "He's being such an asshole to me," she whispers, nodding at Leo. And Macy is rattled. "I'm sorry I got you in trouble."

I turn to look at Leo, who is watching me and Macy, and I smile at him. He smiles back. Okay, me and Leo are cool. I forget for a moment that he's being not-nice to her; those dimples are a contact high for me right now.

Macy takes me by the hand, bringing me to sit in the circle, and I glance at Leo, who is now watching as I walk over and sit down exactly where Macy wants me, away from Leo. But also, she folds into Paul Christensen's lap and they start day–making out, which is a surprise to me. I had no idea Paul and Macy were hooking up.

"I don't get why you and Ravi have to work every bloody day," Nate says in a really bad Australian accent as he takes a swig of beer.

"Um, because our parents aren't loaded like yours?" I counter.

"My parents aren't loaded . . ." Nate starts to protest, and Gus cuts him off.

"Dude, your Mom invented the internet; you're rolling in it," Gus blurts out. Nate's mom didn't actually invent the internet, but she was at one of those internet companies right when it went IPO and made bazillions, so, you know, she cashed out in a big, big way.

Nate scowls and says, "Cut it out, mate." Nate doesn't like having his parents' wealth put out there; he's understated about being rich, the way people in Fair Harbor are, like you'd never know it unless someone teases him like I just did, and really, I wasn't being mean, I thought I was being funny, so I feel bad.

I lean over to Nate and apologize and squeeze his arm, and he gives me a fake shove, and I know we're okay. I sometimes forget how sensitive he is because he's always such a show-off.

And then Nate gets up and does his impersonation of Gus surfing, and we're all dying from laughter because Nate is so good at being someone else.

"Wait, wait, guys, let me blow your mind," Macy shouts as she lies on her back in the sand. She puts her palms flat into the sand behind her head and lifts her body to form that yoga pose, wheel, her hair hanging down into the sand.

"Holy shit, Mace, that's fire," Gus calls out to her, and she beams, so proud of herself.

"Kim, Kim, come sit on me!" Macy challenges.

"What? Girl, you're insane," Kim says, adjusting her boobs in her leopard-print string bikini top.

"No, no, come sit on my stomach. Do it! Do it!" Macy orders, and it's like she's the lacrosse team captain rallying her team-mates. Kim looks at me and I shrug, like, I have no idea if this is going to be a disaster or fun, and Kim does it: she puts her butt on Macy's belly, and Macy's body is in an upside-down C shape, supported by her arms and legs, every muscle in her limbs at full throttle.

We all cheer, and everyone, I mean everyone, even Leo, has their phones out. Look at Macy: she can be inverted in the sand and have someone sit on her and still maintain composure. She is simply the center of awesome.

And then Macy, with what looks like complete control, collapses the two of them into the sand, and they roll around, laughing, laughing, laughing.

"Wait, wait, watch this," Kim says and she throws her long arms in the air as she hurls her body forward, doing an actual somersault in the sand, landing on her feet.

We all cheer for her, and Kim is so proud of herself in this moment and she "woo-hoo"s and runs into the water, but it's too cold and she runs back shrieking and then Gus picks her up and carries her back to the water and throws her in anyway and she screams a bunch, but I can tell she's having fun, and it's contagious, the laughter and the breeziness, and I don't even mind Gus—I can see why he's in the bro-circle: he's a goof when he's not being an insult comic.

I really want to sit next to Leo, and sometimes I see him looking at me, but mostly he's watching whoever is the center of the attention. Leo seems different—and more specifically distant—when we're around all our friends than when we're alone, and maybe he's had time to take in my interrogation of him and Alice and he's decided not to be into me, or maybe he's so angry at Macy that he can't stand to be in my presence.

And maybe I'm just reading into things.

I need some air, and I know that's ironic—I am sitting on a beach with the ocean spray at my fingertips—but all this, all this drama with Macy and Leo, and Alice and Leo, it's too much, and it's more than just a *get over it*, it's somehow under my skin. I also need to pee, so I get up, almost solidly confused about which bathroom to use—should I go to Macy's house or should I go home or should I run into town? I don't want to poke Macy and distract her from Paul's face to consult her on my peeing dilemma; I can deal with it on my own.

And Gus says, "Where you going, fat ass?"

I kick some sand at Gus and look furtively at Leo; it's an impulse that's completely foreign to me and yet feels natural.

"Dude, don't speak to her like that," Leo says to Gus.

This is the second time Leo has told one of the boys in our friend group not to me rude to me, and I like it.

Gus shrugs and digs into his bag and pulls out a can of beer and pours it into his empty red Solo cup and ignores Leo.

I walk toward town—I can use the bathroom there—knowing that the Whelans' house, which is obviously closer, would become a sinkhole I won't be able to leave anytime soon, and everyone says some version of "aight," which is heartwarming in its simplicity.

"Hey, Jasmine, wait up," Leo calls after me.

I half turn, in case I'm imagining it to be Leo, when it could be Nate throwing his voice to sound like Leo. And, thankfully, it's him. It's Leo.

"Where you going?" he asks.

"Town." I mean, I'm not going to tell him I have to pee. That's way more information than he needs about my destination.

"You know where I haven't been yet?" Leo asks. I shake my head, because of course I don't actually know where he's been in the time he's been out here. "The Pines. I really want to go. Interested?"

The Pines.

I know just the place.

* * *

We are sitting side by side on a bench on the Fair Harbor dock, waiting for the water taxi. I've peed, and all my beach worry has dissipated. I'm well aware of our thighs touching; it's a thrill to be this close without him knowing its effect on me. Because we're just being dorks on a dock.

"I love what you did with your post this morning. How did you shoot your hand without an assistant?" he asks, and it's clear to me he is referring to himself as the assistant.

"This was a case of ingenuity. I couldn't figure out how to toy with perspective while holding the camera, and it was like, what's that thing people say, when you try something . . ."

"Trial and error?" Leo suggests, as he motions to the water taxi pulling in with his chin.

"Exactly!" I hit him, playfully, excited that I'm bantering about technique. I'm a photographer talking to a real photographer, and I've basically forgotten everything that's ever happened except for what's happening in this moment right now. He's not just a hot guy I have a lust-crush on; he's someone that likes what I like, color and filters and frame, which for me, who geeks out on those things, is pretty epic.

We are standing on the edge of the dock watching the water taxi gently pull into its port, waiting for the deckhand to moor the boat so we can board.

"So, what exactly did Macy do that you're so angry at her for?" I ask, knowing that this could ruin our adventure to the Pines.

Leo winces. "You really want to know?"

I nod, because, like, of course I do—why else would I ask? "Well, Alice's parents rented that house on Birch—"

"I didn't realize she's also on Birch," I interrupt. Now it makes sense why we see Alice so much; she's Macy's neighbor.

"And, like, Macy came to Alice's house. And I was there. Literally ending things, you know, being clear that we aren't, you know? And then Macy—I guess she was going to the beach—she sees us on the deck talking, and she starts yelling at Alice to stay away from me, or else. Who says *or else*?" Leo pauses. "I got stuck consoling Al, when all I've been trying to do was end things, so that, you know, I could just, like, hang out with you."

There is so much to unpack here. I need to process what he's just told me, but there's also this: he wants to hang out with me.

"You want to hang out with me?" Despite everything he's just said, this is all I hear.

"I mean, yeah," Leo says as he motions for me to get on the water taxi.

I don't have a chance to ask a follow-up question because we jump on the water taxi and sit in the back, where we'll be able to feel the ocean spray on our faces and the wind in our hair. Every so often Leo takes a shot of me and we are sitting so close to each other, in the warm air, away from anyone we know, his arm around the back of the boat bench we are sitting upon, basically around my shoulders without touching them. This is not a convenient heart-to-heart talking situation, so I go with the flow and enjoy the ride, all the while, happy feet dancing in my head, Leo wanting to hang out with me. The way I want to hang out with him.

I text Monte that I'm going to be in the Pines in twenty-five minutes (it's a long water taxi ride from Fair Harbor), and he texts back, Go hang out at my pool. I'm at the beach. All I ask is don't go into the house with wet feet and for goodness sake do not leave a sloppy souvenir in my bed.

I laugh at Monte's text, the heaviness of *or else* catching up to me. I look out at the blue bay water surrounding us, this boy beside me, the moisture gathering in my eyes, and I swallow them back, deciding to shut out what happened with Alice and Macy, and instead enjoy Monte's suggestion that I would use his bed for the things I think about all night and day.

· · ·

The Pines has heaps more people living here, with seven hundred homes compared to our four hundred in Fair Harbor. The Pines is where freedom reigns, where pride resides, the place the LGBTQ community calls home (away from home).

Monte's house is nestled near the ocean, cozily surrounded by a wooden fence and dense shrubbery, and like so many of the homes here, has a swimming pool. And because Monte does not want me inside the house other than to pee, I bring us in through the side door that opens onto the backyard, where the pool is, this large kidney-shaped blue ideal, with myriad floats dotting its clear water, lounge chairs lining the deck, and a bar that has every alcohol imaginable, which we are not allowed to touch.

"So we have this whole place to ourselves?" Leo asks, taking photos immediately.

"Basically."

Leo pulls his shirt off, and I have to take a deep breath of whoa at his spectacular wow of a body as he dives right into the pool.

"What are you waiting for?" he asks, splashing water at me as I'm standing at the edge, mentally reviewing what he'll see when I take off my clothes. Will he be grossed out when he sees me in my plaid bikini halter top and black bottoms, totally mismatched, and by my body, which is not a mannequin's body?

"Jasmine . . ." he calls, floating on his back.

I hesitate, nervous, and then mutter, "Fuck it" and jump in, shutting my eyes so I don't have to see his reaction to what I look like, not caring about my hair dye turning the pool shades of pink. Ah, the water is so smooth against my skin. When I come up for air, Leo has jumped onto an inflatable giant white swan. I swim over to and try to topple him, to no avail.

"Is this what you imagined?" I ask him.

"Better," he says and rolls on top of me, capsizing himself, and the two of us play-sink to the bottom.

I open my eyes underwater, and there he is in front of me, his arms almost in slow motion, flying upward.

Every fiber in my body wants to wrap my arms around his torso and hold on to it forever.

· · ·

We're lying on the striped blue and bluer lounge chairs, side by side, drinking iced teas in tumblers on the deck, completely relaxed except for the occasional interruption from one of our friends FaceTiming me.

"Your friends are obsessed with you," he jokes. "Like, do they always call this much?"

"Well, technically, it's FaceTiming," I answer, and he laughs as I adjust my bikini top.

"Do you think you could stop moving, Jasmine," Leo says more than asks, and I get it, that's Leo-speak for *I'm about to take a photo of you with my 'droid.* I roll onto my side so that I'm facing him, and he takes some shots, and I'm less in my head than when he was taking pictures of me the other night on the deck. "I'm going to post this one on my Insta," he says.

"You need my approval if you're going to do that," I say, and I am not joking. Of course, he takes great photos, but I wouldn't mind weighing in on what he chooses. "You know, I'm wondering about these captions of yours."

"Oh yeah? I'm a poet, but no one knows it," he says, and we laugh.

I seriously want to reach over and begin the kissing portion of this afternoon, but I'm not forward, not like that. I wish I were. I bet I wouldn't have been friend-zoned so many times if I'd just made the first move, once.

"Even though, you know, I had so little swagger as a five-year-old that I'm completely forgotten," he jokes.

"Oh, you mean how I'm your *first bathtub buddy* and your *first kiss*? I mean, okay, according to you, we took baths together, but are you *my* first kiss?" Which, the second I ask this, I cringe. What a dumb question. I should know who my first kiss was. I thought it was Kim. But maybe it was Leo?

"I'm not sure if I'm your first kiss, but you're mine." And he blushes and he doesn't look at me, and he says, "And you're my first girlfriend."

"How do you remember so far back? This is what's frustrating to me. I have zero memory of us as kids. How do you know what was happening between us as five-year-olds?"

"My mom has all these photo albums of me and my brother and they're all labeled, like FIRE ISLAND 2004 and stuff. And there are all these shots of us, me and you, here in Fire Island. Like I could do a short film that I narrate called *Falalala 2004* based on it, you know what I mean?" Leo is animated now, sitting up, speaking in quick bursts, as he recounts our lives to me. Lives I don't remember, not the way he does, which is in living color. "And look at you. You're so beautiful and awesome, how could I forget?"

I can't handle him right now.

I'm beautiful? Wait, he said I was "*so* beautiful." Me. I don't think of myself as "*so* beautiful," or even "beautiful." I think of Macy as beautiful and Adera as very beautiful, while Kim is hot, and I'm more just a girl with a nose and eyes and mouth and it fits on my face and when people walk by they don't look at me a second time, and other than Mom and some of her friends, no one has ever praised my face in any way close to this.

"Jasmine?"

"Yeah, yeah, you forgot to mention how cool I am," I joke, and he laughs.

The joke is easier than the truth for now. I don't know how to say out loud all the things I am feeling, a soaring of my body and heart and being connected to him in this way that's not just about his dimples but so much more, this history that exists outside my own awareness but is there anyway. The dimples appear as we hold a gaze, and it's too much for me, too much, and I look down, I look down like a fool, and yet I am the embodiment of fireworks, heart ones and moony-eyed ones and ones that spell out, LEO LIKES JAZZ, and OMG LEO I LIKE YOU TOO.

We sit in a moment's silence, refusing to ruin it with more words, other than the returning interruption of FaceTiming; this time it's Mom. Which I am required by mom law to answer.

"Hey, Monte tells me you're freeloading," she says, giving me a view of just the upper part of her forehead and her hair as she walks around our house.

"Yeah."

"I'd like you to be home for sunset. And can you stop by their market and pick me up a pound of the kale Caesar salad? I'll Venmo you the cash, okay?"

"Yes, Mom." Like, why couldn't she have texted?

We "love you," and I hang up. I put the phone down and exhale, the wearied sigh of a daughter turned into her mother's TaskRabbit.

Leo laughs as he leans toward me and takes my hand. And I'm waiting for him to get on one knee and propose when he swoops me up in his arms and jumps with the two of us into the pool together, where we chase each other until we are interrupted by Monte.

There are just way too many adults in my life right now.

*   *   *

On the water taxi ride back to Fair Harbor, the sun is starting to shift, the sky drawing stripes of orange and pink across it, and we sit, again in the back, the ocean spray anointing this heart that is us, him leaning into me, and Leo puts his hand on my knee, electrifying my innards. It's so exquisite I almost swallow my whole mouth.

* * *

Mom and me and Leo are sitting on the deck eating one of Mom's staple meals—grilled burgers—with a side of white rice that Burt taught her to make yesterday in the rice cooker, plus the kale Caesar salad I got for her. And she is sitting right next to Leo with her phone out, scrolling through his Instagram, and in particular commenting on the photos he has taken of me.

"Mom, seriously, stop," I say for the twelve hundredth time.

Leo laughs as he eats a second burger. "Jasmine, Cooper's throwing a free tonight. You wanna go?"

And before I can stop the words flying out of my dumb mouth, I ask, "Oh, can I invite Macy?" His smile freezes. "I know she's not your favorite person right now . . ."

"Wait, Leo, why is Macy not your favorite person? She's like a second daughter to me," Mom asks, interrupting her Jazz-picture fawn fest.

"Ah, it's complicated, Ms. Jacobson," Leo says, trying not to get sucked into Mom's vortex of interrogation. And I feel guilty for not having thought about Macy until right now.

"Leo, I'm Ms. Jacobson at school. You can call me Ava, okay?"

"*Mom.* Please. You're being—"

"I asked Leo a question, Jazzy," Mom cuts me off.

"Well, Ms. . . . I mean, Ava, it's just, it's . . ."

"Mom, leave us alone, already," I say, joking but also not joking, but also trying to help Leo out of total awkwardness.

"Okay, okay, okay. Wow, Leo, this photo you have of Jazz on your Instagram is so gorgeous," Mom says, back at Leo's Insta, and it makes me cringe, that Mom is looking at them.

"*Mom!* Can you stop stalking Leo's Insta? That's so creepy."

But Leo laughs. "She looks amazing, doesn't she?"

"Oh, honey, you really captured my daughter." And the two of them gush over all his Insta posts of me, and I just put an imaginary pillow over my face until they quit it. "Do you think you could take a portrait of us? I would really like that."

"Of course I can, Ava." Leo smiles as he charms the cranky out of Mom.

Mom starts to clean up the table and Leo cuts her off, saying, "Ava, let me clean up." I get up to help, and he motions for me to stay put. "I'm your guest, so I'm clearing the table."

Mom leans across the table, turning her body a little so she can see where Leo is, and she whispers, "There is no doubt in my mind that that boy likes you, Jazz."

And my heart burps again, because if there's someone that can read people well, it's my mom, so I know what she's saying comes with credibility and, of course, now I want to hear more of what she has to say about Leo liking me. "You think, Mom?"

"The way he sees you through his lens, honey. That's really special. That and the way he looks at you in real life. That's always the telltale sign, child of mine."

Sometimes, I just want to hug Mom, and this is one of those times, but I don't, because weird.

* * *

Adera is walking in front of our house along the bay, and Mom sees her before Leo or I do, because we're looking at some photos he took on his phone of seagulls, which sounds boring, but with his eye, they are anything but, their white bodies in silhouettes against the sun; they're simply majestic.

"Hey," we all say at once.

Adera bounds up the wide steps to our deck and sits next to Mom. "Ava, are you coming to sunset with us?" she asks, her hair in long, loose braids with golden cuffs hugging them.

"Should I come out to play?" Mom jokes, and I'm like, *Please, Mom, stop, you're not funny,* but I don't say it out loud, I'm not going to get into a fight with Mom in front of Leo—no way.

Of course, my friends encourage her to come to sunset. And Leo stands up and mutters something about the light, then tells me to sit next to Mom and takes a bunch of photos of me and Mom as she puts her tiny arms around me. And then Adera decides she wants a photo taken too.

"Can we go upstairs?" she asks, and I think that's a great idea.

"Okay, I'm going to change while you guys do your photo shoot. Let's leave here in ten minutes, because the sun is going to set pretty soon," Mom says in her bossy way.

And then Leo says, "You know what? I'm going to run home and get my camera. Cool?"

And I smile at Leo for confirming with me that it's cool he goes home. I like that.

"Okay, see you at sunset!" Adera and I toodle-oo him away.

I grab my camera, and we run up the staircase to the upper deck, and Adera chooses her spot, literally exactly where Leo took those moonlit shots of me. Adera strikes a pose, arching her back, her long yellow dress against the blue of the cushion, legs crossed at the ankle, her arms up, a halo around her head.

"So, what happened when you guys walked off? Did you hook up?" Adera asks as we cruise into our shoot.

"No! Can you believe? We jumped into a pool, and he did not try to kiss me. At all!" Adera is more experienced than I am with boys—all my friends are—so I know whatever her point of view is, it's going to be spot-on.

"Hmmm. That boy is so strange," Adera jokes.

"Can you pull your shoulders back? Wait, what?"

"He's spending all this alone time in *daylight* with you. And he's not trying to mash with you? That's not a boy trying to be your friend, that's a boy who likes you. I mean, he's sitting out there with your mom." Adera stands up, readjusts her dress, which has been riding up, and then sits again.

"Can I ask you something, and if I do, can you swear to cone of silence?" I ask, and Adera, of course, is a vault of secrets, but I have to lay down the rules, that this stays between us. "Leo told me Macy showed up at Alice's and kind of threatened her. Did you know about that?"

Adera's mouth hangs open, and it's clear to me she is in shock. "Aw, girl, no. Tell me it's not true."

"It's what he said. Macy saw them together, got super protective of me, and then went Mama Bear on *her*." I pause. "I feel sort of worried for Macy. And I blame Max Cooper."

"What does Max have to do with it?"

"Adera. She's still . . . she's still hung up on him. I think it's messing with her, this crush she has on him. She gets mad so easily, like this thing with Alice." I'm almost in tears, and it's a sudden rush; I've been holding on to this anxiety, and now saying it all out loud is making me see how real it is.

Adera sits beside me and puts her arm around me.

"Whatever is happening with Macy, honey, that's going deeper than him. Like, I backslid into Lyndon, and that happened twice, and I know, I know, I don't like the way he is with me, and by the way, I'm done with that noise, but it's not making me go extreme, you hear me?"

The words Adera utters settle into me, mixing with the wash of worry and the line of logic as I assemble the pieces.

And everything she says makes sense: it's not Max Cooper's fault that Macy was walking along Birch, saw Alice Adams talking to Leo, and then went *or else* on them, it's on Macy. I swallow, and realize I forgot to ask Adera an important question. "Why did you cut it off with Lyndon?"

"He ghosted me. Plus, he gets rough when we're mashing. I don't like it."

I nod. Because what do I know about rough mashing? Not one thing.

•   •   •

The dock is packed.

Adera and I snake our way to our friends. I spot Macy's mom, Olive, talking to Burt and Miho, but I don't want to speak to her; she's the worst in her sarong and her butterfly ankle bracelet, so I avoid my housemates. Mom is with Nate's parents, and there's a woman standing with them and she looks just like Nate's mom and I figure she's Leo's mom, the twin sister. Wow. I do a lap, looking for Leo, but I don't see him—he's not with his family—and so we continue to thread our way through the crowd. Every single person that could possibly be in Fair Harbor is here, like three hundred and ninety-nine households decided tonight's the night to be at the dock.

We finally find Nate and Gus and Kim and Macy and Paul, who has his arm around Macy's neck, like hanging on to her, at the very edge of the dock, and it's a relief to see my whole friend group out here. Things are getting back to normal.

"Yay, Jazzy's here," Macy announces and wraps her arms around me, smelling like vanilla.

And as she folds around me, I pull her close, close where she'll be safe, attached to me. I spot Leo, about ten feet away, standing by the water taxi stop, where he and I were only four hours ago, and he is with Alice and her friend group. My stomach roils, my face prunes—seeing them together is a lot—and Macy catches me watching them and grabs my hand and pulls me away from the world I'm living in, toward Crabby's, where it's less busy.

"Let's go for a ride," Macy says.

Macy wants to go for a ride. To Saltaire. That's what she means.

"I'm not in the mood," I say, also being a best friend, looking out for Macy, not indulging the impulse to ride by Max Cooper's house.

Macy frowns at me. "Don't worry about Alice. I'll take care of it. She's had her final warning."

And now I immediately regret stressing about Alice in front of Macy—how stupid of me.

"Mace. You do not do a thing to Alice Adams. You hear me? I like Leo, and I don't want drama, and anything you say or do to Alice Adams will cause drama for me."

"Boo. Did he even try to kiss you today, Jazz? Max made it clear he was into me when—"

"No." But here is what I know: Leo Burke is not Max Cooper. Leo Burke is probably not a rough masher. Leo Burke is a boy that cites me as his first girlfriend. He's not like these idiot boys.

"See? He doesn't really like-like you. You're in the friend zone. So forget about him and let's go for a ride," Macy says quickly, with a theory opposite of Adera's. And by the way, I prefer Adera's take on my afternoon with Leo, not Macy's.

"You're being mean, Macy."

"I'm just telling you what you don't want to hear. I mean, look at her. She could be a model. You're just . . . cute. Do the math."

One minute she is threatening to do something terrible to this girl who likes Leo the way I do and the next minute, she's fat-shaming me.

I take a deep breath. I don't have words that can protect me; I don't want to put up with not-nice Macy, and I don't want to watch Leo talking to Alice even though he says they are not involved, and I tell Macy I have to pee, so I slip away and go to the bathroom in El Muelle because Woodson's is closed now and I splash some water on my face and push the tears back into my brain and fix my eyeliner, and these are the times in my life when I say to myself, *What Would Jazz Jacobson, World-Famous Photographer, Do?*

You know what she would do? She'd be a badass and she'd not be feeling jealous and she'd be in the middle of the Fair Harbor social scene with her camera, looking for shots to take. Meaning: she'd face everything and not back down.

Even though it's still crowded, I make my way back to the end of the dock. It takes me a few minutes—there are so many people here—but eventually I get to Nate, and he is with Adera and Kim and Macy and Paul. Gus too. Plus, now, thankfully, Leo is with everyone plus some girls from the town of Lonelyville but not Alice anymore, and that means that whatever was happening ten feet away from me ten minutes ago is now over.

And they're all talking about going to Max Cooper's free later, and Leo is standing there in his vintage yellow Beastie Boys T-shirt, the Leica around his neck, his jeans worn in with a tear on one of the knees. He is watching me and he smiles and I smile back, calmly, but inside I'm melting.

We "hey" each other as I place my whole body next to his. "You waiting for someone?"

"I was thinking about it, Jasmine," he says, emphasizing the "Jasmine" part, which, I get it, he means, he's been waiting for me, and I smile, a smile for the world to see. He flips his body around so he's facing me, his back to our friends now.

Gus shouts, "Yo, Burke, not cool, man," and Leo laughs. He puts the Leica to his face and takes a photo of me, explaining that the way the light is hitting me right now needs to be captured forever.

And then Nate says in an announcer-type voice, "Looks like your mom made an appearance, Jazz Jacobson."

And Leo spins back around and I look over at Mom, who is walking with Nate's parents and other people's parents, and I say, "Yeah, you know, us Jacobsons are social butterflies."

And then Leo says, "You know that's my mom your mom is talking to."

"I bet those two are planning your wedding," Nate says, still sounding like an announcer, and then everyone starts making stupid kissing sounds and humming "Here Comes the Bride," and Leo laughs and I tell them all to shut up and someone says something about Leo posting a photo of five-year-old me.

Wait, what? I pull out my phone and if you were to look at our friend group, you'd see a whole bunch of teenagers all looking at our phones, looking at the same photo, a mini Jazz in pigtails and a purple bikini with chocolate ice cream adorning my cheeks, a mini Leo behind me, his arms around my waist, his little muppet head over my shoulder.

Oh. My. God. The cuteness, but also: This is our history. This is what Leo's been referring to. This is what Leo remembers, this feeling right here, of two little kids in an embrace of endless love. Okay, maybe that last part is me hoping that's what he's remembering.

"So, yeah, I have a whole lot to show you," Leo confesses to me, and only to me, which I love, that we're in our little bubble, miles away from everyone around us. Plus, I can't wait to see the rest of the little Jazz photos.

Kim pulls out her phone and shrieks, "Wait, what? Jazz, how cute are you??!" and she screenshots it and puts in on her Insta story and so do Adera and Macy, referring to me as a "Takeover."

"Leo, you've been cuffed to our girl your whole lives," Kim says, and everyone except for me and Leo—who turns six shades of intense—starts laughing.

We all start to walk away from the adults at the dock, and we wave at Ravi, who is at work at Crabby's, and we walk toward the beach and all end up huddled by the lifeguard chair on Birch. I make a point to sit next to Leo, even ordering Nate to make room for me, because he's practically in Leo's lap.

Somebody breaks out a vape and passes it around. Me and Leo don't have any, and then someone lights up a joint and that gets passed around too. I notice Leo's 'droid is buzzing and he checks it and I lean over to peek—well, really, I'm snooping—and now my shoulder and his are touching and he looks at me looking at his text and it's Alice asking where he is and he doesn't write back.

"Hi," he says. And I guess that's his way of not talking about Alice.

"Seriously?" I demand. "Okay, so, questions: Weren't you just talking to her at the dock? What did she want?"

"She was like, 'I need closure.'" He shakes his head. "So I listened to what she said, and that means she had her closure. I think we're cool now."

I've heard that one before. Macy on Max Cooper, now Leo on Alice Adams. Thinking things are cool when they're breaking someone's heart.

"Cool as in . . ."

"Like, I don't think we're going to be friends, but I think she gets we are not ever going to be anything else, and she got to say that she's mad about it," Leo says it very quickly, and I get it, it's uncomfortable, but I am happy he is being honest with me.

And I feel like I'm ready to shove off this topic.

"So, you think our moms are BFF now?" I mean, I'd rather ask more questions about Alice, but I can tell it's not what he wants to talk about, and this is what I guess is a compromise: he told me stuff; now I ought to listen to other things on his mind.

"Maybe. Wanna see what I didn't post?" I mean, of course I want to see this other version of us, our little kid selves. Leo shows me a picture of the two of us naked at the shoreline, sitting with our backs to the camera, our little butts perched on a dinosaur float, and I feel my cheeks turn red, and he puts his arm around me and leans into me, whispering in my ear, "See? We should have done this at Monte's."

I cough because I'm already imagining us trying to skinny-dip, and I wish someone would throw something at me so I could stop dying of awkwardness.

* * *

It's about ten, and Macy and I are riding our bikes to Max Cooper's free, the humidity so thick it feels like riding through a pile of dough. Macy and I are singing "Ding-Dong! The Witch Is Dead," for no reason and not caring that our voices are out of tune. The bike racks at Max Cooper's are full, so we just leave our bikes on the grass with all the other bikes that are not in the racks.

"How do I look?" Macy asks, and honestly, she looks better than I've ever seen her, her strapless denim bustier giving her breasts this soft mushy valley, her belly shimmering from the gold bronzer she spread on it, her shorts so short her legs seem longer than my whole body, her hair pulled back in a high ponytail, pink glitter gloss on her lips.

"I mean, gorgeous." I don't ask how I look; it's not a competition. However, my hair is bomb because Macy touched up the pink—we did a pre-party dye job, we had to, because jumping into Monte's pool was not the smartest move on freshly dyed hair. I basically just put on jeans, and she lent me this pink sheer gauze shirt, and my hoodie is shoved in my basket, because it's too hot to wear. "Please be chill, Macy."

"What? Why are you being so weird?" Macy asks, and, yes, maybe I'm being a little extra, but I'm worried about her. "You still worried Leo is mad at you because of some goof I pulled? Fuck that dude."

"I like him, Macy."

"And I like Max Cooper, but you know, you're always reminding me what a dick he is, so . . ." She bites her lip. Maybe she sees my face, even in the darkness of Saltaire at night, fall into splinters. "Ah, Jazz, I'm sorry, I'm just amped up."

"Mace? Maybe we should just, like, not be here. Like, Max Cooper's girlfriend might be here. You going to be okay with that?"

"Of course I am. Me and Max have our secret language. See, I didn't even need your help. I figured it out on my own."

"Figured what out?" I ask, worried that what she's figured out isn't actually real.

"That I just have to be here, waiting for him." Macy smiles, flinging her arm around my shoulder as I absorb what she's telling me. "I love you, Jazzy. Let's go have fun, okay?"

She's not going to listen to me if I push back; she just wants to go to the party, and so do I. I want to meet up with Leo. I just need to be here for her, and I roll with it, excited about what's at the end of this long gravel path up to Max Cooper's, the music blaring, people walking by us with red Solo cups in their hands.

I've been at Max Cooper's a hundred times, but I'm always surprised at how it feels bigger on the inside, like the TARDIS, these walls of glass that seem to rise into the sky, everything bathed in a warm light. Max Cooper's house is teeming with people, Mac Miller blaring, and I can't hear my thoughts; this party has way more people than last week's party did.

Did a ferry bring all of Long Island to Max Cooper's house?

"Yes, girl, you finally showed up," Adera says, hugging both of us. I'm not sure which one of us she's referring to, but I'm thankful to see someone I know, even though Adera is there with a guy I don't recognize at all.

Macy tells us she'll be right back, and we all know she's going to look for Max Cooper. Adera puts a hand on my shoulder and squeezes it as Macy disappears into this endless sea of bodies. I appreciate the wordlessness of the moment.

"Have you seen Leo?" I ask Adera.

"Text him. He's here somewhere."

Adera is right, so I text him, but because he has a 'droid, I have no idea if he got it. Whatever, I am not going to find him standing in one place. I start to thread my way through people, "excuse me"ing as I walk around, doing some version of an S-shaped lap, and it's so hot in here, I head out to the wrap-around deck, where the ocean breeze cools me down.

"Look who it is!" Benga exclaims, shirtless, his buff body flexing every muscle that exists on it, his white shorts a size too small on him.

I "hey" him and I'm wrestling with whether to ask if he's seen Leo when a blond girl "woo-hoo"s her way into Benga's sightline and he winks at me as he goes back inside. I stand on the deck and lean against the rail, taking everything in through the glass wall that separates me and fun: all these people, dancing and drinking, and it feels so good to watch it, and then I see Leo, talking to Alice, by the kitchen.

Leo, talking to Alice.

Again.

Like they were earlier at the dock.

What is *happening* here? It bothers me to see them together, even though I know he likes me. I don't like that I'm a jealous girl. I don't like that I'm wondering what to do, interrupt them or wait for them to finish talking. I don't like that anytime I am not around, he is with her.

Without second-guessing myself, I take a photo of it. Because I want to know that I'm not imagining what I'm seeing. And I really, really don't like who I am right now, this girl, worried.

They're standing super close, her hand on his waist. He's holding a red Solo cup with one hand, and his other hand is in his pocket, and every so often he leans forward to hear whatever it is she's saying, and her mouth is moving really fast but I cannot tell if she's telling him a story or telling him off or telling him she wants him in her life.

I'm absolutely unable to do anything except swallow and watch, knowing he can't see me from inside the well-lit living room. Every so often he looks around, but otherwise, he's just standing in the midst of a bajillion people and only talking to Alice. A part of me wants to text him, but what if he looks at his phone and ignores my text?

"Look, it's our social butterfly!" Ravi says, interrupting me, a red Solo cup in his hand too, and this guy standing with him, another guy I don't know.

I'm so relieved to see Ravi. Something, anything to distract me from watching Leo Burke talking to Alice Adams.

"Hi!" I turn my body so that I'm facing Ravi directly and so Leo is out of my sightline.

"Julian, this is one of my best friends in the whole world, Jazz." Ravi is being weirdly formal, and Julian smiles, his teeth gleaming, his very dark hair pulled back into a ponytail. He's got a choker made of shells on his neck, and he is, like so many boys here, shirtless, buff like Benga.

"I've heard so much about you," he says, hugging me without me understanding why. And then it clicks: this must be the boy Ravi hooked up with, the boy Ravi likes.

"Julian!" I gush, the proud friend that I am, so excited for Ravi.

"Why you out here by yourself?" Ravi asks, standing a little too close to me. I mean, it's, like, encroaching on personal space.

"I was inside, but it's so loud and hot, and also, I lost Macy."

"I haven't seen her," Ravi says.

"Yeah, we came together," I tell them. And then, I can't help it, I turn around to see what Leo is doing, and he's not where he was, in the kitchen with Alice. In fact, neither one of them are there. And I want to start a search party. Instead, I try to be a conversationalist by asking, "So what's up?"

"We lost everyone the second we got here," Ravi says and laughs, and he and Julian smile at each other.

"Julian, what town are you at?" I ask, grammatically incorrect.

"Oh, my parents have a place in Lonelyville. It's our first summer here," Julian says, pointing to the party. "They would *not* be down with this mess; never ever would they let me throw a party, not here, not in the city, not anywhere."

And I can't take it anymore. I can't make small talk. "Ravs, can you do me a solid and text Leo and tell him I'm out here?"

"Um, bossy much?" Ravi says, but doesn't hesitate, his fingers racing across his phone. "Voilà! Now he knows."

I see Nate walking toward the deck, or at least, I think he is, but in fact, he walks right into the glass wall, grabs his head, and sits down. Julian and Ravi start laughing uncontrollably. We watch Kim run up to Nate, put her arm around him, cradling him as he gathers his wits.

"I see a love connection happening here," Julian comments.

"There's no way. Those two?" I say, wondering where the hell Leo is.

And then Macy bounds onto the deck, her cheeks brimming with tears, and Julian runs up to her. "What's going on, girl? Tell Papa Juli." And this is when I notice that Julian is really tall. Macy's body gets swallowed into his as Ravi and I crowd around her, all asking her some variation of "What's wrong?"

"Max told me to leave," she says as she starts to cry.

And we all respond with a "What the . . . ?"

"I, I found him in his room, I don't know why I thought to look for him there, and I hugged him and I thought we were about to make out and he told me, he literally told me I was being crazy!" Macy stands up. "Me, crazy?"

"Why would you just, like, find him in his bedroom, Macy?" I ask.

"What? Why are you asking me that? Did you not hear how he spoke to me? He called me crazy!" Macy yells.

I look at Julian and Ravi, who are so busy taking care of her they don't see me. I turn to the party again and see Max Cooper with his arm around his actual girlfriend, Tina, and a bunch of people around them doing shots.

Of course he wants Macy to leave. Bringing her here was a terrible, terrible idea.

"Jazzy, give me your phone. My battery died," Macy demands. I hand her my phone, and of course she knows my pass code; we're best friends. I am sure she's texting one of her rando dudes, and I don't have a problem with a rebound hookup; I'd like to dive into that myself right about now. If I had hookup options, which I don't.

Julian and Ravi exchange looks. "You know what? Let's go for a ride to the Atlantique docks and have our own party there," Julian suggests.

I want to do whatever we can to possibly distract Macy, and Atlantique is remote enough to keep us far enough away from here. "Yes, let's get out of here, okay?"

"I just don't understand why Max was so mean to me . . ." Macy says, and starts crying again.

And Julian just swoops in with "Girl, we can't have your beautiful face sullied by those tears. Begone, tears, begone!" He waves an imaginary magic wand, and Macy starts laughing because Julian—and by the way, I am so into Julian and Ravi right now, and I bet I will be for always, maybe I'll just refer to them as Javi—is our hero.

And even though I've been waiting here for Leo my whole damn life, Macy needs me right now, and I push Leo out of my head—like, what is taking him so long to come to the outer deck, where I am?—and we rush Macy out of Max Cooper's house and into another dimension: the marina park that is Atlantique.

•   •   •

"Let's sneak onto one of these yachts," Macy suggests, her mood much lighter now after the fifteen-minute bike ride and ten-minute walk through the sandy path to Atlantique's marina, which is basically a parking lot for yachts.

"Now, remember, if we get caught, it will not be a fun night, but whatever, I'm game," Julian says, looking to Ravi for backup.

"Do you think we'll get in trouble?" I ask as we crouch-walk along the dock, looking for a boat to be badass on.

"Yeah, bro, let's go," Ravi agrees wholeheartedly, and then it's just me, the basic girl sitting steadfastedly on a basic fence.

"Chill, Jazz. I did this all the time last summer," Macy reassures me, and I hush, trusting in the edge of my rule-breaking ability. Macy has been sneaking onto yachts for a while, although I have always been too nervous to do it with her, plus she had sex with Max Cooper here last summer, twice.

Most of those boats here are owned by people who live on the mainland in the town of Islip, and they come over to Atlantique and stay here or in Lonelyville for a week or two. Atlantique's version of town is the Shack—basically, their Crabby's—and the public restrooms, and of course, the Atlantique Marina.

I remember as a kid, Mom or Gayle would bring me and Macy to the Shack to get ice cream; it was always an adventure leaving Fair Harbor to eat ice cream in another town. We'd walk toward the bay, then romp about in the children's playground while Mom stared wistfully at the paddleball courts, watching the shirtless men swatting at balls.

"Here, this one," Macy says, leading the charge to a yacht that's nestled into a slip sandwiched between larger yachts at the end of the dock. This boat is called *Don's Draper*, and has a snazzy U-shaped wood veneer bench at its stern.

Macy climbs onto *Don's Draper* first, and then Julian and Ravi jump on in tandem. Ravi turns to see where I am, unsure if I'm following Macy into a post-traumatic rabbit hole or if I'm just being a baby. I reach into my back pocket for my phone to see if Leo's texted, and then I remember Macy has my phone.

"Jazzy, snap out of it," Ravi says. "You're going get spotted." Ravi's right, the longer I stand out here, the likelier it is that someone who may be walking a dog or trying to do what we're doing sees me standing here like a dummy.

"This is so much better than that shit show Cooper called a party," Julian tells us.

Not one of us is drunk, and yet, all four of us are lounging like we own this boat, taking hits off Julian's vaporizer, the sky illuminated by the stars, and the occasional interruption of the ferry cruising into the marina.

"Aw, shit, Burke just texted," Ravi tells us. My heart leaps. *Yay.*

"Mace, has he texted me?" I ask, watching her take a hundred selfies of herself with my phone.

"Nope. Aww, Moo. Fuck that dude," Macy tells me. And then my heart drops, because she's right, I need to be fierce in my disappointment. He was standing talking to Alice, *again*.

Like, how much closure do two people who were not official need?

And then I realize how insensitive it is of me to think that, when my very best friend is going through the same thing with Max Cooper.

Yeah, fuck that dude, I want to say, but instead stay silent because we're finally relaxed, and Macy is far from Max Cooper. I turn away and look at the water, not letting anyone see how upset I am, that I wish I were with Leo right now instead of them. I want to believe in Leo and believe in the day we had, and I want to forget what I saw, and because I am fighting both sides of my brain, I will myself to not think about him.

It's a superpower I developed when I became a girl who got friend-zoned, ghosted, and, in general, rendered invisible by boys I have crushed on. Helps with avoiding nights like this.

Saturday
Two Days before
the Fourth of July

Chapter Five

I wake up and instinctively reach for my phone, hoping, hoping that Leo has texted. And there's still nothing. I check to see if the Wi-Fi is working, and then I see that the little airplane, right next to the Wi-Fi bars, is active. *I'm in airplane mode? How did I do that? When did I do that?* I don't drink, so I can't blame it on alcohol. I was stoned, but I get loopy when I smoke weed, not self-sabotage-y. I switch my phone back to send-me-all-the-texts mode, and then, in a blink, there they are, stacked green bubbles, filled with Leo Burke.

WYA?

Are you here?

Adera says you are here?

WYA?

Did I do something?

Today was epic. I like being in another town with you.

Wait, Ravi says you're in Atlantique. Where? Can I come meet you?

You know what? You're probably not getting these. I'm going to DM you.

Still nothing. Jasmine? Jassssssssmine!!!

I missed you tonight.

I missed you tonight.

Good night Jasmine. 🖤

There are no notifications from any of my socials popping up. I go to my settings, and the notifications are off. But I always have them on. I check my Insta DMs, and there are messages from Leo there. My heart does a Snoopy dance: Leo was texting and DMing, and he was trying to meet up with me! All. Night. Longish.

How did my phone betray me? I look at Mom, sleeping only a few feet away. She knows better than to mess with my phone; she knows she'd be starting a war. The only person who could have done this is . . . Macy.

Dots are connecting, and I don't like the pattern of them.

I return to the DMs, and look at the time stamps, and they started coming in around ten thirty, about the time Macy took my phone. She had my phone from the second I saw her on the deck until we biked back to my house, and then she went home.

Even though I know Adera is asleep, I text her: Leo was looking for me? Please confirm?

I brush my teeth in the shower, dry myself off on the deck, and get dressed. My mind is spinning. It's too hot already even for a shirt, so I just wear my bikini top and denim skirt, and I take my gear and my notebook and slide my feet into my flip-flops and walk down Fifth Walk to the beach, the sun making its way to its throne in the sky, the air still thick with humidity. It's going to be as warm as it was yesterday, possibly warmer, and it's all good because as I stand at the top of the steps, I see him.

Elation and relief engulf me.

Leo is waiting for me on the white sand, white from the glory of the sky's shine—those blue, blue skies. My toes get lost in the sand as we start walking toward each other in slow motion, his hoodie unzipped, no shirt underneath, his Hasselblad at his side. We are in sync as we stop at each other's bodies, almost touching.

"Hey," he says, and I raise my chin to meet his eyes and I can't speak. I am in a trance of glee, I can see that he is as well, I can see it in the way his dimples outshine the sky, the way he inhales as we come a step closer to each other. He puts his hands on my face, and I'm not sure for a minute what to do, so I put my hands on the bare skin at his waist, and his eyes close for just a moment, and I pull him toward me, and he bends down, our minds joined at our lips.

"Jasmine, Jasmine," he whispers, and it's a softness that my heart celebrates, and my eyes are open—I don't want to miss a moment of this, his hair falling into our faces as we spend our eternity in this moment, our first adult kiss.

Interrupted by a big brown Labrador licking my leg.

Both of us laugh, that nervous laughter acknowledging what just happened and, at the same time, we bend down to touch the dog, its owner apologizing, the two of them melting away from us, and Leo and I look at each other.

"So . . ." I say. I am nervous, and I've never felt like this before, and I don't know exactly what the pinpoint of my feeling is, only that every fiber of me is in a state of a smile.

"I lost my mind a little last night," he tells me.

Me too, I want to tell him, but I only have a short window of time and more questions than God. "Why?"

"I thought you were pissed at me. Adera said you were at Cooper's, and then Ravi said you were all on the deck and I couldn't find you and then you weren't answering my texts. I started DMing and you weren't answering those either. Or opening my Snaps. I thought you were done with me." He moves his hair from his face, the dry wind blowing us into each other. "I was not expecting this!" He laughs as he pulls me close to him again, and we're kissing, kissing like this is our thing, has always been our thing.

I laugh. "I'm surprised too." I'm relieved we were both wanting to see each other. I'm annoyed that it's a possibility that my best friend got in the way of that. And I'm gleed out that we've just had our first kiss. "Leo. Listen. I have this theory so I'm going to have to ask you to go with me on this. And it is so crazy, but can I see the texts? I just need to look at the time stamps."

Leo's face falls blank, and then confused, and then he taps in the pass code to his 'droid (ugh, this 'droid), and opens up Instagram, and his DMs, and there they are, like ten or more, all starting at about the time we were at Max Cooper's. WYA?s and Ravi says you're in Atlantique, and Can we meet up? and WYA? and HMU? and WYA? and Are you mad at me? and Jasmine?

The silent scream swells within as suspicion curdles into a truth. He was trying to reach me. And Macy sabotaged it. I look up at Leo.

"What, Jasmine, what?"

"I don't know if I can tell you," I start, wanting to protect Macy, my instinct is to do that, always, even as kids when she'd spill her ice cream off her cone and Olive would flip and I'd take the blame for it so Olive would chill. And the tears flood my eyes, and I can't believe we've just had our first kiss and now he's seeing me cry. Ugh, I'm the worst. And if I tell him what I suspect, he's going to be even more pissed at Macy than he already is.

"Jasmine? What's wrong?" Leo leans in, placing his fingers gently on my face, moving the tears away, into the air, and kisses me again.

Kissing him is an energy boost.

I'm such a whirlwind of mixed feelings, I fling myself onto him with such a force we fall backward into the sand, our cameras cursing us as we make up for all the time our lips have been apart, my body sinking into his, his hands wrapped around my bare string-bikinied back, and it's like I'm an expert and have been doing this forever, with Leo.

"Leo," I start, knowing everything I am about to tell him is going to ruin everything that just happened.

My alarm clock goes off, which means I have forty minutes to get home, upload, post, get to work. I reset my alarm for ten more minutes from now.

"At the party I saw you with Alice, while I was on the deck. And then Macy came out and she was upset about Max

Cooper and her phone was dead, so I gave her my phone, and after that, I didn't get any notifications."

"Wait, what? Did Macy block me?" he asks. And our bodies are no longer intertwined; he's sitting up, and all the sweetness has morphed into something engineered by Macy. "And wait. You saw what?"

He falls back into the sand and rolls us to our sides, and we are each where the other is in our adoration, hands on each other's faces, in each other's hair, cameras at our sides.

"I have to shoot my frames," I whisper between kisses and legs wrapped around each other's.

"I wasn't thinking that at all." He laughs, and, well, he doesn't have to tell me that. I can feel what he's thinking.

But.

I don't have a lot of time, and I still have fifty frames to click off, and now my camera might have sand on or in it.

"Listen. I have to do my photos. Can we agree to be angry and then talk about everything later?"

"Only if it means we can do more of this," he says, rolling me onto my back, sand now finding new grooves in my skin, and I wonder how Macy could ever have sex in the sand; I can barely lie in it for five seconds.

My phone alarm dings again.

Thank goodness Leo, as a fellow photographer, gets my plight, that I have to disentangle and get to work, despite how bad I feel or how angry he is with Macy as he rattles off all the texts he sent. The sky beckons, wonder and sunshine awaiting in my fifty frames, this sky full of pink streaks and cotton-candy clouds.

"Hey, do you think I could use your hands today?" I ask him, an idea that I am coming up with on the spot—unusual for me; I preproduce this shoot every day before I step onto the sand—my set—but something about the way our fingers are braided in one another inspires me to pivot.

"Uh, this sounds like a fetish," he jokes, and I raise our arms into the sky and take my fifty frames with my left hand in his right, clasped against the horizon. I'll have to update my notebook with today's creative when I get home.

And then Leo takes a selfie with the two of us in the frame. How he does it with his beautiful and now sand-filled Hasselblad, I have no idea, and we head back to the house, our fingers intertwined in each other's hearts.

Best Day Ever.

#supportwomen #photography #jazzmatazz #summerproject #iphoneX #macmiller

Today's post is a photo of us holding hands, his nails crooked and bitten, my nails short and a little brittle, with the sky so crisp behind us, almost appearing like a blue screen. I don't think I have ever held a boy's hand and documented it, and in some ways, it's the most important personal photo I have taken yet.

• • •

I have to share, not on Finsta, but here, in text, the biggest moment of my life with my girlfriends.

it happened. We kissed.

KIM: Now that's what I'm talking about!

MACY: tell me everything

ADERA: Girrrrrrl!

I'm basically considering this my first ever adult kiss.

KIM: You cannot count kissing me when you were 11 as a first kiss.

MACY: LOL.

ADERA: How was it?

Oh my God. Better than Jim and Pam. Better than Spiderman and Mary Jane. Better than The Doctor and Rose Tyler.

ADERA: Who are The Doctor and Rose Tyler?

The most romantic couple of the whole Doctor Who series!

ADERA: Leo was asking about you last night. Confirming that btw.

KIM: Yeah, he was spinning.

Well, so today, Leo was waiting for me at Fifth, and BOOM! It happened.

MACY: Are you exclusive now? Or is this a hookup?

It doesn't feel like a hookup. It feels intense.

MACY: So psyched for you!

ADERA: OUR GIRL IS A WOMAN NOW

LOL

Two minutes later, Macy texts, a sidebar, one that doesn't include Kim and Adera:

> Why did I have to find out on a group chat?

I don't answer because I don't argue in text.
And I have a lot to say to Macy right now.

· · ·

It's about eleven thirty in the morning, and the heat is unrelenting and flat, worse in this shack with its heavy smell of coffee and dirty soap water, even with all my sanitizing and wiping. I am serving ice cream and other food that people order when it's this hot, ice in everything, and trying to hold on to this morning, the first-kiss part.

"What are you looking at?" Sue snaps at me, catching me watching her from my perch at this counter, wondering what life would be like if I could just take her two hands, like women do in period pieces like *Bridgerton* and *Emma*, and say, *Oh my, the most wonderful thing happened this morning!*

"You got customers, kid," she adds, highly agitated today; the humidity has turned her body into an unresolvable mush, and she can't wipe the perspiration fast enough.

I tear myself away from watching Sue at the grill and turn to face my least-favorite customers: Alice and her friends. And even though she does not know I had my first kiss with

Leo this morning, she absolutely *does* know that she won't be the girl he is kissing anymore. I'm relieved when it's Sekiya who does the ordering for the group.

"Can we get four iced coffees, please?" Sekiya asks, her shades on, her smile resplendent. Still, it is clear that this is a business transaction and I am here to serve, and we won't be exchanging further tips on lip gloss.

"Make sure there's no milk in mine," Alice snaps as I turn to prep the drinks.

Alice is always rude to me, but today it's tinged with a meanness, and I am not here for it. I lean forward on the counter, elbows supporting me. "Having a tough day?"

Alice rolls her eyes at me and crosses her arms in front of her chest as Sekiya pays. And then I get to work prepping the drinks, and Sue wipes her hands with a towel and flicks her chin at me; Sue, who is witness to every second of my ass jiggle but also, my drama.

"What the *h-e*-double-hockey-sticks is up with all these customers today?" she mutters, Sue's version of her absolute approval of how I handled Alice just now.

Sometimes, Sue is the best at giving me what I need in the moment.

●　●　●

I'm still high-fiving myself with how I dealt with Alice when Leo shows up at the counter, alone. Him being here is so welcome; his incandescent beauty soothes the sting of knowing what Macy got up to.

"Hey," Leo says, so casually, like we just saw each other five minutes ago, which I guess we sort of have—he's been liking every one of my photos for the last hour, and he leans over the counter and puts his hands on my cheeks and holds me for a moment before we lean in toward each other. "I've been thinking about it, and I want to say: I'm really sorry about last night."

Sue, ever the lurker, catches us faster than the kiss lasts. "Hey, hey, hey, get a room," she fake-yells and Leo pulls away from my face, laughing.

"Hi, Sue, happy to show you the love too!"

We both laugh as she scowls.

"How're you doing, Leo?"

"I'm having the best day ever," he says. "Can I get a Rocky Road on a sugar cone, no sprinkles, please?" He winks at Sue and she laughs, knowing he's just placing an order so he can stay.

"Coming right up."

"So, you? Decent day?" Leo asks.

"You know it started off pleasantly enough," I joke, because of course we know that it was almost the best, well, the part of us kissing, that is. I want to tell him about Alice giving me shade, but I know it will invite more drama. "My customers, though? Rude. And now I'm replaying all of it in my head."

"Ha, I do that. Like dissect every word someone said to me," he says softly, like he is feeling my pain and gets that I'm having a hard time, and I feel the burden of my confession ease up.

"It was Alice, by the way," I blurt as I hand him his ice cream cone. I lost my internal non-drama battle. "She was my rude customer."

And Leo purses his lips, clearly annoyed. "I'm sorry. Do you want me to say something to her?"

"What? No. I took care of it." I would prefer if Leo never even said hi to her, but, you know, I can't dictate his every move, and I don't want to. "Don't worry, I didn't tell Macy about it." It's a half joke, but also a half not-joke. "But I will be talking to her about what she did with my phone."

"Okay. Let me know how it goes," he says as he leans in and kisses me, quickly, before Sue catches us again. Leo's phone buzzes, and he looks at it, sucks in his cheeks, and then puts his phone back in his pocket. "Gotta go. Nate says the waves are going off. But I'll see you later, like sunset time, okay?"

"Yeah, cool," I tell him.

Because sunset is a thing and so are we.

* * *

Ravi arrives, and I follow him into the back while Sue remains out front, tending to customers while we do our shift turnover. He's wearing the same Childish Gambino T-shirt he had on last night, so maybe he never went home?

"So, Julian?" I ask, leaning against the wall.

"Yeah, Julian. I have been trying to get at you. So. Finally. I have my first actual boyfriend." He laughs.

"Yeah, I'm sorry. I'm sorry I've been so . . ." I hug him. "I'm happy for you, Ravs."

"Hold on, sis, I'm not getting married. I'm just taken," Ravi tells me, with the added bonus of a gentle squeeze on the fleshy part of my upper arm.

When we were eleven, there was a boy, Devin Bright, and Ravi followed him everywhere in Fire Island, to the point that even Nate felt left out of their bro hangs, and I remember Macy saying she thought Ravi was in love with that kid, but it was just an offhand thing to say. I didn't know that it was something else, something real and beautiful and flourishing within him. That came later.

"Great. I love you, Ravs."

"Look at us two, finally with boyfriends." Ravi glows at me. "It's our summer, Jazzy, our summer."

"Wait, how do you—"

"Dude, you know we're all tight, right?" He laughs as he walks out, winking at me.

* * *

I text Macy: WYA.

Saltaire. Meet at yours?

I don't like that she's in Saltaire, but I hit her back with a thumbs-up and I go home.

* * *

Mom isn't home, and I'm dealing with an *Oh, you have to eat something* Burt, a cranky Miho, and a napping-on-the-couch Theresa.

"Hey, sunshine," Burt chirps as I walk into the kitchen to get a bottle of Coca-Cola, his Sade playing softly so as not to disturb his sister. That she can sleep anywhere has always seemed like an enviable talent to me.

I grunt, and he scowls at me. Fine, I get it, he wants an utterance packed with words. I smile brightly. "Do you know where my mom is?"

"Yeah, I sent her to pick up some tuna in Saltaire."

"Excellent. I'm going to sit on the deck and ignore you people," I half joke but really mostly mean.

Burt rolls his eyes at me as I walk out onto the deck, spray myself with sunscreen, pop in my AirPods, and lie back on the chaise lounge, losing myself in *Blonde* by Frank Ocean with my eyes closed, but I'm not asleep; I'm really giving this relaxing thing a go while I wait for Macy.

"*Jasmine!*" she says. "Take out those pods. I have so much to tell you!"

Macy is wearing a white bikini top and a pair of cutoffs, and a gold cross sits below her clavicle, almost like an amulet, and she seems to have gotten tanner and more gorgeous overnight. I grab my phone and shoot ten frames as she grabs her boobs and arches her back and lifts her legs, playing the part of pinup for me and my lens.

I can be mad as mad can be and still take photos of her.

We'll get through this.

I stop taking pictures. I am ready to confront her about messing with my phone.

"Now listen to me," she says and just as she's about to speak, Burt steps out on the deck and tells Macy to come in and eat if she wants to and we both "uh-huh" him and then he steps back into the house. "I hooked up with Kieran Granger last night." She juts out her phone, the proof that they were together is right in front of me, a selfie of her and Kieran at 2:20 last night, darkness a blanket around their faces, the flash obliterating all else. I don't have to wonder how good she is at hooking up: look at her, so confident, so gorgeous, so much fun.

"Was this after we were in Atlantique?"

I mean. We were on *Don's Draper* until about midnight. So it's possible she did something after we said goodbye. Kieran is a waiter at El Muelle. And in . . . *college.* "Wait, isn't he like twenty-five?" And I stop because I hear how stupid I sound and I have more important things to discuss with her.

"No, silly. He's a rising junior at Georgetown, so . . ."

"What about Paul Christensen?" I ask. I'm starting to lose track of the boys she's been hooking up with, just as I'm losing control of this conversation.

"Oh, that? That isn't anything."

"So sex was had?" I laugh. How amazing would it be to have sex with Leo, though? I blush at the thought, and thankfully the sun is glaring in Macy's eyes and she can't see my whole body react to my runaway thoughts.

"Indeed. On the beach!" We both start laughing.

"You probably don't even notice the sand in your butt anymore from all the beach hookups you have."

"Also, wait," Macy says as she catches her breath. "I have a bone to pick with you. Is it okay with you when big things happen that I get the tea first?"

"Aww, Mace, it was just easier to tell all three of you at the same time," I explain, again getting sidetracked.

Macy bites her lip. "I'd just rather you tell me first and then the group. Okay?"

I shrug. She wants to know things before I tell other people? Our friends? Fine. It's not a big deal. But also, I need to get back to the bigger problem here. I bite my lip because what I'm about to say can't be unsaid. "When you were on my phone last night, did you change my notifications?"

"Wait, what?" Macy asks.

"Did you put my phone into airplane mode deliberately, when you knew I was waiting for Leo to text me back?" I sit for a moment, waiting for her to answer. But she doesn't. She sits in silence. A damning admission. "You made it impossible for us to connect. Controlling my evening, like I'm some puck in a lacrosse game!"

"It's not a puck; that's hockey. We use—"

"Macy!"

"I just needed you to be there for me, okay? I had to do that so that you wouldn't disappear on me for a boy." Macy pauses, allowing the guilt attack to wash over me. "I'm sorry, Moo. It won't happen again."

I want to tell her I will always be here for her, but I can't find the words, I'm so angry at her. So angry. "I like this boy, you know, Macy?"

Macy leans back on the chaise lounge beside me, putting her sunglasses on, taking the sun in. She reaches over and holds my hand, squeezing it as she talks. "Okay? I'm sorry. Look. Last night was a lot. I snuck back into Max's free," Macy tells me, burying the truth in a laundry list of my thing/her thing. "I mean, that's where I found Kieran."

And it's like I was there. She hooked up with Kieran deliberately to have sex at the part of the beach that is at the end of the walk that Max lives on, on the off chance he would walk to that part of the beach at that hour of the night and become enraged with jealousy.

This is the fantasy of the hopeful.

"But Max Cooper legit threw you out of his house, Macy.

You can't be sneaking into his frees and having sex on the beach with randos in front of his house."

"Max just doesn't realize we belong together. I have to help him get there. Actually, you said you'd help me come up with ways to convince him I'm his The One, and you haven't yet." Macy is seamlessly weaving one drama into another, and I'm just trying to make sense of us; that's all I want.

What is going on with Macy, really? I think about the constant and deliberate rides into Saltaire, particularly riding up to Max Cooper's house, and Macy being above-average aggressive, and the day drinking, and all these rando guys—it's all weird, weird stuff that I've never seen Macy do before, and I'm afraid for her.

"I don't want to, Macy, because I think there is no winning Max Cooper back. I don't think he's your person. I don't think it's worth our time. You have to get over Max Cooper, and you have to do it, like, yesterday." Not only am I upset about what she did to keep me and Leo apart, but now I'm upset that she's not letting go of her idea of Max Cooper, of this impossible dream of being with him. "All of this, this stuff you're doing, this is just, it's not you, Macy."

"Don't, Jazz. Just don't." Macy raises her voice, which is surprising; she's never done that with me before. I've heard her yell at people, but never me. It's more than intimidating; it's scary to me. So. I back down. I back down so hard, I should just rescind my membership as a friend in society. Macy frowns, throwing her towel at me with that lacrosse stick swinging arm of hers, and it lands with a wallop. "Listen, Jazz, don't give me a reason not to believe in you anymore." Macy throws the punch into my gut, shutting me up. "It's like this thing with you believing Leo over me—"

"Enough, Macy, enough!" I raise my voice too, just like she did.

I don't even recognize myself right now. I have never yelled at Macy before; the world itself feels like it's skipping a beat.

We sit in silence for a long time; I know I'm not going to get closure from Macy on this. I have to decide right now: let it go or keep at it. Both are shitty options. I wait to speak, until I can say anything in a way that I won't be ugly crying or ugly talking. I stand up. I love Macy. I don't love this side of Macy. And we have never had an argument, and I'm not sure how to make this go away. "I have an idea."

"But we're not done . . ."

"Yes, yes, yes, we are. We're going to put a pause on this and we're going to go get the inflatable boat and float in the bay."

"But look at the clouds. It's going to rain soon," Macy protests.

"Since when are we afraid of rain, Mace?" I wink, and Macy laughs.

We are, for now, thawed out. She's the Macy that I fell in love with when we were ten, bouncing around in the bay, squealing every time seaweed wrapped around our ankles, splashing at each other without caring about anything except for when we were going to Crabby's for ice cream.

Calm washes over me, topped with a sash of a smile.

We may still be in an argument, but if we just zone out for a bit, we can just be who we are.

*   *   *

The shaking of my shoulder is increasing with ridiculousness, and I open my eyes, and Mom is sitting on my bed, speaking my name, behind her the window to a rainstorm crashing upon Fire Island.

"You okay, pups?"

I can count the number of times I've napped in Fair Harbor: it's never.

"*Mom*, go away."

"You need to get up, Jazzy."

"What? No! Why? Mom. I'm *tired*. Work was so stressful, and I have sunset in a little while," I moan as I try to roll over, knowing sunset is going to be canceled. I can hear thunder, the crackle of lightning in the distance, and the sound of the rain coming down.

Mom bites her lip; she seems to find the fact that Crabby's can be stressful a joke, and I kind of yell *"Mom"* at her, and she says, "Okay, okay, what is going on?"

And of course, she knows that whatever is bothering me is either Macy-related or Leo-related not because she is a telepath but because she's been listening to me talk about both of them all week, and so I choose not to tell her that I'm worried about and also angry at Macy.

"Leo kissed me today, Mom," I say, not wanting to dive into the quagmire of Macy.

"Jazzy, how wonderful!" Mom pauses a moment, thinking what she could say, and cups my cheek with her palm. "Well, I have good news for you."

I sit up—if I don't pay attention now, she will never leave. And she's smiling, smiling my worries away. And I roll my eyes so she can see that I am not enjoying her smiling at me.

"Okay, fine, don't play along. We are supposed to be at El Muelle at six forty-five for dinner with Emily Burke and her son, Leo. So you can sit here in your drool or you can get your butt in the shower, because we are going on a mom double date."

A mom double date?

"But don't you not-like Emily Burke?" I ask, because, like, hello, Mom was ghosted by Leo's mom.

"Honey, that was a long time ago. And Leo is clearly old enough to decide who to have playdates with," Mom jokes, and it's the most cringeworthy joke ever. "Okay, full disclosure: Emily reached out, set this whole thing up. So come on."

Normally I would hate this idea, but it means we're seeing Leo, and that will make this angry pile of bagels in my belly dissipate.

* * *

Under the table our legs are entwined while our hands busy themselves with the feeding of this meal. Leo and I spend the whole dinner answering questions ("Where do you think you'll go to college?") and dodging questions ("What do you kids do out here every night?"), and the moms brag about how Leo and I are both photographers, and we avoid talking too much to each other because we both know that the moms will read into every word we say. I'm pretty sure, although he hasn't said as much, that Leo probably doesn't tell his mom every detail of his life, and so anything we say would be ammunition for her to ask him more about stuff he doesn't want her to know. The moms gossip about people they knew ages ago in Fair Harbor and also, stop talking every single time me and Leo speak directly to each other, like they're snooping on us in front of us, a totally suave mom-squared move.

Leo orders steak, the moms each have roast chicken, and I go for the pasta. It's fancy, but so is El Muelle, and this is a double date after all. Leo's mom drinks a whole bottle of red wine, while Mom works a glass of iced tea, and Leo and I drink iced teas and sometimes our waters.

So it's a long two hours, and my phone is buzzing the whole time, mostly text messages from Macy and the rest of our friends, but I can't read any of them because the rule with Mom is that I'm not allowed to use my phone when we're eating, and that includes breakfast, lunch, and dinner, and she's super strict about her rule. But then we're done and the moms decide to have coffee and they tell us we don't have to listen to them anymore and we are out of there so fast.

That was a very long two hours.

"Your mom hugs a lot," Leo says, as we exhale our way away from them.

"Yes, tell that to my rib cage . . ." I joke, which makes Leo laugh so hard, water emerges from his beautiful eyes.

*　　*　　*

We walk out to the dock in the rain, no one is out, obviously, and Leo is holding the umbrella, and we are pressed up next to each other as we walk to the end of the dock, at sunset hour, even though there is no sun tonight, just a sky with water pellets.

Leo puts the umbrella on the wet wood floor, even though it is raining. He holds my face, the same way he did this morning, and this time, I place my hands on his, holding us in place, and the warm tears from above fall upon my face and because I am on the precipice of an ugly cry, I lift myself up to my tiptoes and I kiss Leo first—I make the first move, me, Jazz Jacobson takes control.

"Jasmine?" he asks between our kisses. "My pants are so soaked, my legs are basically floating in them."

The rain is now coming down in sheets of madness, and Leo grabs the umbrella, his arm around my shoulder, protective of me, my heart swelling for him with every step. He's completely soaked on the left side of his body—this umbrella isn't wide enough to cover two people—and I'm paying attention to the wooden boardwalk—it's slippery when it's wet, and I don't mind because I'm this close to him and so safe.

*　*　*

The housemates have gone to El Muelle to hang with the moms, so we have the house to ourselves. Although there's not much we can do other than wait for the adults to get home, because when they do, they'll be interrupting whatever it is we are doing. And really, my brain is too timid to consider the options of opportunity too closely.

"Do you want to borrow something of Burt's?" I ask Leo as he sits down on the couch, swimming in his soaked pants.

"Nah. But would you mind giving me a towel and throwing my jeans in the dryer?"

Leo, on my couch, in a towel, only a towel? This is an option? That won't get me in trouble if we're interrupted by Mom? "I'll be right back," I tell him and I go upstairs, to my room.

Despite Leo keeping me covered by the umbrella, my pants are also wet. I change into a cute black halter-top maxi dress and put a zippered hoodie on too in case he catches on that this is not what I wear casually around the house. And even though he said he wants a towel, I choose my plaid robe, which is long enough on me that it won't be too short on him, and then I go back downstairs.

Leo is standing by the sliding glass door, watching the rain splatter onto the deck, a puddle of water at his feet. As I hand him the robe, I wonder if he's cold. "Actually, do you want to take a shower? It might warm you up."

"Wait, is that a legit offer?" He smiles widely and pulls his wet shirt off, which, you know, momentarily stuns me, I don't think I will get used to seeing Leo without a shirt and not react in a way that is basically a full-body blush.

"Yes, of course it is." I take his shirt from his hands and bring it to the sink in the kitchen, wringing it out a little, and Leo follows me, exactly the way I always follow Macy: without hesitation.

"Okay, let's go!" He grabs my hand and starts walking to the deck out in the back, where the outdoor shower is.

"Wait, what? No, I mean, *you* take a shower to warm up." Oh my God, if Mom came home and found us in the shower, she would be on my grill for the rest of the century.

Leo starts laughing and puts his arms around me. "I had to try."

He picks up the robe, which he'd left on the couch as he followed me about, and drapes it on, sliding off his pants right in front of my face, the way surfers do at the beach, getting in and out of their wet suits with, like, towels draped around their waists.

"Sure you won't take a shower with me . . . ?" he asks as he heads to the outdoor shower, which is an excellent place to shower in the rain, the hot water pouring from the spout as cool rainwater surrounds you—ah, it's epic.

"Go away," I joke, even though we both know that the only place I want to be is in that outdoor shower with him.

* * *

I'm deep into an Instagram troll when he returns into the house, in my robe, his hair wet, his face glowing.

"Jasmine." Leo says my name, and I am going to hurl myself across this sunken living room and kiss his face, and I stay where I am because if I sit next to him, we will kiss, and my mom will walk in, and if she saw me kissing Leo everything would be ruined because she'd be awkward, so I just sit here, oceans away.

"Can I come sit next to you?"

I pat the spot beside me, and Leo smiles, a really big smile, and it's like neither one of us is nervous or weird anymore, and he comes and sits exactly where I want him.

"You know when you said this morning that you lost your mind last night?" I ask him.

"Uh-huh," he answers, his face on mine.

"I had the same experience, I think, when I watched you talking to Alice, and that's why we all left—well, that, plus Max Cooper kicked Macy out," I say, and it feels emotional, like I will cry, being this honest; it's scary, but also, I'm replaying that moment last night when I had to literally shut my feelings down or I would just die, before I knew Macy had sabotaged us being together.

"You have to believe me when I tell you that Alice was a hookup and the operative word is 'was' and honestly I thought she'd had closure at the dock, and I was waiting for you at Cooper's. Remember? I went home to drop off my camera and you went to Macy's and we were supposed to meet up at the free? Like, I had a whole plan of how we were going to have our first kiss: I was going to walk home with you along the beach, and I wanted to kiss you there, or, like, where we did this morning, but at night. You feel me, Jasmine?"

I put my hand on his chest, the patter of his heart confirming everything he's said, his presence beside me the answer to any questions.

"Did Macy tell you what happened with Cooper? In his room?" Leo asks.

I know that whatever he is about to tell me will be something I won't be able to unknow, something about Macy, and I am now aware that dread does not suit me. "Um. Not really."

"He went into his room to get his guitar, and she was already there sitting on his bed. And then he told her she needed to leave, and she just sat there. He's really freaked out. And today, he told us that he thinks she took his cross, that gold necklace he wears." Leo stops talking for a moment. "So you didn't know any of this?"

"No." I don't think I can hear another word, and I know too that today, she was wearing a gold cross around her neck that I now know is not hers. "Leo, I'm worried about her. Like, messing with my phone and stalking Max Cooper, and it's just, it's just a lot."

I stand up and start to pace. If it weren't raining so hard right now, I'd suggest pulling the inflatable boat out and escaping.

"Jasmine, maybe you should, like, talk to her about it."

"I mean, I have been." I bite my lip, in an effort not to cry again. "Leo. She's been my best friend for a lot of my life. So I'm trying to understand what is going on with her. This is not who she is."

"Jasmine. She's hung up on Cooper, and she's watching you be with me."

"Is it really that basic?" I ask, even though I know the answer; she literally told me as much today, that Leo is just in the way. That she doesn't like it when I don't tell her things first. That I don't have her back.

"It is that basic," he says definitively.

Well, tomorrow, we're going to have a straight-up talk, and maybe I can help her get over Max Cooper, instead of just yelling at her to do it.

I'm going to be a better friend.

* * *

Leo DMs me. Yes, it's now 2:38 a.m., but we're both awake. Wide awake, in my case.

Look at what I did.

And he attaches a link to his perma Insta story, and in the almost hour since we said goodbye, curled up in each other on the couch until the adults spoiled our quiet time, Leo has posted photos into his stories folder of us from the summer of 2006. I recognize my little punk-ass face, and I'm literally doing flips in my head, seeing this world I was a part of but don't remember.

Me, in mini! I have so many questions

Save them for tomorrow!

I would like to keep texting him, but I resist. I have to wake up early to shoot *Galentines*. And that also means I'll be seeing Leo, at the beach, early in the morning. So I put my phone on its charger and close my eyes.

For about three minutes. Then I go back to his permanent Insta story and there's another photo there, new. It's of five-year-old me, sitting in the lifeguard chair at the bay. I have on a purple bathing suit with yellow polka dots and my hair is in pigtails and my bangs are long and my face is one big smile and the caption says, *This is my girl*, and he credits his dad for taking the photo and. Wait.

This is my girl.

My heart hiccups.

I'm his girl? Is this really happening?

I can't put my phone away, my index finger almost burning itself out, swiping and liking and rewatching and rewatching. Every photo is newly uploaded, and every caption is adorable, like, *How did I let her slip away?* under the photo of the two of us holding hands, up to our ankles in a bright blue kiddie pool, and I'm wearing the same bathing suit in all these pictures and, like, what, Mom couldn't buy me a few bathing suits? Leo writes *Isn't she lovely?* under the photo of my five-year-old face covered in sand, with him holding out a clump for me. I guess he was going to put more on my face, whatever, kids are weird, but their faces and body language are so expressive, and these two mini versions of us are telling me a whole story, a story of love and of dreams and of life.

The Day after
the Fourth of July

Chapter Six

We are up at the same time, me and Leo, his DM and text coming in at exactly 6:35 a.m., we doing this? The sky seems angry today, on the verge of a possible storm, the bay water high against the shoreline in front of my house. When Mom and I first got here a few weeks ago, the weather was like this too, wild and petulant, and Mom and I had to lay sandbags in front of the house to keep the bay water from flooding the property.

Is Nate coming? I ask, because that was something discussed, that Nate would be surfing with Leo this morning.

Nate's definitely coming.

I respond with a shrug emoji and rush through my routine, excited for my morning with Leo, plus Nate. Apparently, the waves will be "going off," which is surfer-speak for *Let's not give Jazz and Leo any alone time ever.*

This weather is a gift for a photographer shooting a series on the beach: the sky is a chiaroscuro of grays and whites and the ocean a blue so dark it reads black, capped with the white ruffles of ocean spray, simply exquisite, and there, on those waves, are two boys on surfboards, milking the short curls of water, having the most fun ever. Weather like this is an invitation to surfers and photographers, not a deterrent, that is for sure.

I have my raincoat on and several lens cloths at the ready to wipe away raindrops and ocean spray. I go to the very edge of the moving target that is the shoreline, where the incoming tide meets the sand that I stand on, where each time the water approaches, I retreat just a bit, as I worry about riptides and sharks, even at the depth of where my toes may be slightly immersed.

I am so mesmerized by Leo, on his board, waving at me every single time he pops up to catch a wave, his black wet suit almost turning him into a silhouette in this light, his wet hair in tendrils helicoptering around his head with each movement. How brave is Leo, to be in that ocean with all the sharks lurking? It occurs to me he needs a lookout, someone to yell, "Shark!" in the event a fin appears and he's unaware, and I could be that person, and I should tell him exactly that after this surf session is over. I hesitate to get on with my day—I am still on borrowed time before work begins—so I spot him for a bit and then get to work.

The two of them being at sea, so to speak, gives me a chance to shoot my shots without distraction. The light is white-gray bright, and it's a challenge to avoid the pitfalls of overexposure, the rain heavy at times, but I don't mind any of these obstacles; this is practice for when I'm in the world outside of here. I place the Barbies—yes, they are back—in the sand, standing, facing the ocean, arms raised. This is the epitome of a *Galentines* post: two girls, basking in their lives here at the beach.

Sound ceases, except for Leo's voice hooting at the waves. The dolls are so fragile in my hands, and my eyes blur, my throat suddenly dry.

Macy.

I wipe my eyes, my nose too—it's starting to run—and I put my gear away, looking toward the houses, where the clouds seem to be changing color, from their ominous grays to just ashy white, an indication that the rain will stop soon, which is a relief. I notice two figures standing on the deck of Nate's house—which I have yet to be inside of this whole time hanging out, although, of course, I've been over to Nate's a million times over the millions of summers we've been coming here—arms folded across their chests, mirror images of each other. I raise my hand to them, a wave, and only one of them waves back.

Probably Nate's mom.

How weird that Emily Burke doesn't, but maybe she doesn't see me. Whatever. I already have a mom whose moods I navigate around; I don't need to stress about Leo's. I sling my stuff over my shoulder, spin around, and return to the shoreline, taking shots of Leo and Nate on their boards, although most of my photos are of Leo.

Because of course they are.

> ### I'll Always Be There
> #sondheim #supportwomen #photography #jazzmatazz #summerproject

It was hard to choose a shot—so many of them did what I wanted them to, these two Barbies, side by side, their backs to the camera, arms raised, facing the challenging surf before them. *I have your back, Macy*, it says, *I have your back*. And I tag her, because I want her to see it.

And start talking to me.

• • •

The rain has stopped, and the sky is slowly opening up, blues peeking behind the grays, humidity thick again. Ravi will be starting at noon because it's so busy, and he'll be doing that for the next few days. Still no word on when we're getting a third person in here. I did a double yesterday, on the actual Fourth of July; I feel like a hero for it. This is what busy season is like at Crabby's—tonight we'll be open until eight forty-five.

My first customers of the day, my very first ones, at 8:02 a.m., are Max Cooper, Benga, and Evan, all three of them drenched in dewy coats of sweat, shirtless (do these guys even know what a T-shirt looks like?), and in their shorts; clearly they've been running.

"You're here early." I can't help but say the obvious, as they stand panting at my counter.

"We're training for the marathon," Evan says.

"And it gets hot after nine," Benga explains.

"Thanks for explaining summer to me, Benga," I joke, as if I don't know how hot it gets when the sun is in the sky. "Okay, so what can I get you?"

All three of them order iced teas, and then Benga and Evan walk into Woodson's, leaving me alone with Max Cooper. He is not wearing a gold cross on a gold chain around his tanned neck. I get to work so I don't have to look at sweaty blond hair flat against his large head atop his wiry body.

"Hey, listen, I'm worried about Macy," Max Cooper says in a raised voice, making sure I hear him as I work. Why is Max Cooper saying words at me right now as I approach the counter with the drinks? "You have no idea what's been going down."

He is right; I have no idea. I haven't even seen her since before July 4. She hasn't opened my Snaps or answered my texts and she hasn't liked any of my Instagram posts and she hasn't walked by Crabby's. Basically, she is avoiding me.

There's a distance between us, and I am unable to step toward her, bridging the space.

"Wait, Max. Have you found your gold necklace yet?" I just need to hear it from him. That it's missing. Because I know exactly where it was a few days ago.

Max Cooper shakes his head. "Nah, but if you know where it is, I'd appreciate knowing and—" he starts and I interrupt him. I do not want to be the one who confirms for Max Cooper that Macy has his gold cross necklace.

"She's not over you, you know."

"Jazz, I know that. We're just friends. It's not anything other than that, and it hasn't been," Max says quietly.

I feel Sue's hand on my back, gentle and calm. "Son?" This one word actually sounds like twelve hundred *go away*s; it's sinister and low, with all the authority of an angry parent, itching to bestow the punishment of a lifetime.

Max Cooper does exactly what Sue intends: he backs up, taking his iced teas with him.

"You know, I have never liked that kid. He's always been a rude-ass punk," Sue says, and then then she does the absolute worst thing: she messes my hair up, as if we are friends who are playful and enjoy each other.

· · ·

In the bathroom, I stare at the portrait I took of Macy the other day, a gleaming gold cross languishing on her chest.

* * *

A few hours later, Kim's whole family—her two dads and her kajillion brothers—stop by Crabby's, and all seven of them want the exact same thing: double scoops of Rocky Road on wafer cones, chocolate sprinkles—and I swear, I think my nose is frozen from the amount of times my body is in the freezer for this family, scooping to the point that my right arm is feeling like an overcooked noodle.

Still, all this testosterone is lovely. Particularly because Kim's dads are so happy to see me, and Sue doesn't seem to mind them hugging me over the counter, these majestically tall men, raising boys plus Kim.

"Have you spoken to Macy today?" Kim asks.

"No." I shake my head, aware of the breathing dragon that is Sue lurking.

"Yeah, last night wasn't pretty." Kim pays for her family's cones, which allows us this brief moment to exchange tea.

"What are you talking about?" After work, I was too wiped to do anything with my friends, but we're not really hanging out together obsessively like every summer of my life, giddy with independence from our parents. Everyone is doing their own thing, or maybe even nothing at all.

Like, Leo and I just hung out at my house, which was great because the adults were at a party. We turned off all the lights and watched the bay from the couch, our limbs enmeshed in the dark, careful and alert in case Mom showed up, and all of this is new for me, and all of it is welcome. We had actual privacy, which is not usually possible in Fair Harbor unless you climb up onto the lifeguard chair.

"I'll tell you later. But listen to me: it's getting messy with Macy. We need to, like, have an intervention, before she does something that's really, really not okay."

I blink. Because that's a lot of vague information I don't know what to do with.

Also: a pang of guilt. That I've not been fixing us.

"*Kim*, let's go!" Thing Three calls.

Kim and I pledge to catch up later. I turn to look at Sue, who is standing a foot away from me, her hands on her hips, her brow furrowed. "Listen to me, today is going to be *busy*. I get it, you got some drama outside this shack. But when you're in this shack, you are drama-free, you got me? And how many times do I need to tell you to sanitize the counter!"

Ugh, another freaking lecture from Sue. Like I need that ever.

"Now, don't pull that face, Jazz. I get it. But today? Just work. Got it?"

I nod. Sue is usually cranky, but this is something else. This is: concern.

Not typical for Sue.

• • •

I don't like what Kim said, because it leaves room for me to make something up, filling with worry. I text Macy again:

> Is everything okay?

No response.

• • •

Ravi comes bouncing into Crabby's, putting his surfboard in the back, his hair wet and filled with sand, immediately setting off Sue, who's already crabby because it's been so hectic, and she barks at him to get it together, as soon as possible.

"Yo, yo, yo," Ravi singsongs into my ear. "So you've got Burke whipped."

"You. Are. Gross," I poke at him with each word. Also: What is he talking about? Do these dummies consider hanging out with the girl you like (me) as "whipped"? Idiots. "Have you seen Macy?"

"Nah, Julian and I went to the Pines last night. We literally fell asleep in a bubble bath somewhere." He's glowing, *fully* taken with Julian, totally. And he's calling Leo whipped. Ahem.

"I had this thought, before, like I feel like our whole friend group is kind of going in their own direction," I say as it hits me suddenly, how we're not all on top of one another like we've always been, hanging out at sunset every night and aimlessly wandering around.

Ravi puts his arm around me. "Aw, honey, I'm still here. For you." He pauses. "Also, I saw Alice and her friends getting on the ferry today. So that's my hot goss. You're welcome."

Alice leaving Fire Island is a Christmas in July–level gift. Yes. Now I don't have to feel a pit in my stomach every time her name comes up, or that Alice is trying to corral Leo into another conversation about "what happened." And I don't have to be on the receiving end of those baby-blue side-eyes.

"Ravi, you got sand all over my floor!" Sue shouts at her favorite employee as she comes back to shoo us toward the counter.

Yeah, she's crabby.

. . .

Hey wya, I text Macy.

No response. Again.

. . .

After work, I ride my bike to the end of Birch, park it in the bike rack at the Whelans', and walk down to the beach, where my friends are: Kim, Adera, and Macy.

This summer has been so weird, like all the things that are our rituals—from sunset to the endless bike rides to just, this, hanging out on Birch—have been off-kilter, like we're in some upside-down world. To see these three lying, side by side, house music playing on Adera's phone, facing the ocean, is a relief, the path to normalcy.

"Hey," I say to my friends.

All three of them—Kim sandwiched between Adera and Macy—prop themselves up on their elbows, to "Hey" me back.

Macy too, the cross dangling in the space between her shoulders, a diviner looking for its true master; I force myself not to stare at it. "It's Moo," Macy singsongs, like we're as we've always been, crazy about each other, solid.

I pull my towel out of my bag and settle in beside Macy. "Where's the kid?" I ask Adera.

"The kid has gone back to the mainland for a few days. So I'm freeeee."

"How was work, dear?" Kim asks, like a wifey-poo, on her stomach and sunbathing topless as always.

"Ugh. It wasn't the worst, but damn, are people rude."

"Where's your Lord and Master?" Macy asks, obviously referring to Leo. So there's the rub of her anger too, a reminder of something broken.

"Chasing waves with Nate and Gus," I explain—they're *surfers*, which I get.

Also: I get Leo later, and for as long as I want. Well, at least until bedtime.

"So is that why you're squeezing us in?" Macy asks.

"Hey, hey . . ." I start, trying to come up with a good rebuttal, and then stop, because comebacks are not my talent. Taking photos is my talent. Being a good friend is my talent. Being able to fart incessantly after I eat a burrito is my talent. Being able to come up with a snappy retort? Not so much.

Macy sits up, and it's now that I realize, because her boobs are staring at me, that she's sunbathing topless too; avoiding tan lines is an art form.

"Macy, *cover*!" Gayle's British voice cuts through our tension, reprimanding the show of flesh. Macy raises her hand, a polite Queen's wave, acknowledging Gayle, then puts her bikini top on. I did not realize that Gayle is sitting just ahead of us, keeping an eye on Dylan, who is in the ocean with his friends, as well as spying on Macy.

"So you're hungover? What did you get up to?" I ask, recovering from my inability to be clever, while also trying to be nice. Yes, we have this unresolved elephant of issues between us, we haven't even gone on a bike ride together in two days, basically unprecedented, but I just want to be here. No boys, no distractions, no nasty. So I'm going to be cool.

"No, I *was* hungover. Now I'm just stoned," she says, taking a puff of her vape pen. I look at Adera, and she shrugs.

"We had a wild night," Kim adds, something in her voice catching my attention. "Right, Macy?"

"Depends on your definition of 'wild,'" Macy replies, a little laugh in her tone.

"Okay, let me begin," Kim says, clearly needing to share whatever it is that happened, and she sits up, her bikini top now on, and Adera sits up too, also covered. Because the rules.

"Macy and I were, where else, in Saltaire—"

"Come on, not fair," Macy protests.

"Super fair, because when you say, *Let's go for a ride*, what you mean is, *Let's go see if Max is out*, right?" Kim laughs, her eyes directly on my face, and I get it: this is what has Max Cooper and Kim on edge. "So we're in town, and we see that gorgeous boy hanging out at the gazebo with Evan and Benga, who, did you know he's hooking up with that girl Shira, who went out with Max like two years ago?"

The answer is: I don't remember Shira, and I don't keep track of who Benga hooks up with.

"I didn't know that, by the way," Macy adds, laughing. So clearly, she's not minding Kim telling this story.

"And then, wait, where was I? Oh yeah, so we ride by the gazebo, and this girl sitting on Evan's lap shouts out, 'Oh, look, there's your stalker, Max.' And of course, this bitch is just, she's drunk. And Macy stops her bike. Parks it in the bike rack. Walks up into the gazebo. And says, 'Say that to my face.'"

I look at Macy, and she shrugs. "Gotta protect my name."

"And she goes, to Macy, 'I ain't afraid of you.' And what does our darling Macy do?" Kim's gotten more animated, like she can't stop the words from throwing up out of her mouth.

"She licks her thumbs and puts her thumbs on this girls' forehead. And everyone starts laughing. And then Macy turns and walks away, and the girl comes running down the gazebo, screaming, 'Stalker, stalker,' and pulls on Macy's hair"—and now, now Kim is standing, acting out Macy's movements— "and Macy very calmly lifts this girl up, carries her to the dock, and throws her into the water. Oh my God, I was *dying*."

"Holy shit," me and Adera say at the same time, but neither one of us is laughing.

Macy threw a girl into the water in the bay. I can picture it. I can see Macy lifting someone, even tossing them over her shoulder, to prove a point, to put them in their place, this place of *shut up*.

"Max, obviously, helped the girl out of the water." Kim winks at me.

"And then we went back to Kim's and got wasted. And then I hooked up with Cory." Macy smiles. "Remember Cory Parang?" No. No, I don't. But obviously, a Fire Island boy. "Yeah. So."

And then she has rebound sex?

"You picked up some girl and you threw her into the water," I finally say, but really, I meant to ask, *Why?*

"Gus and them do that all the time to us," Macy shrugs, trying to compare our friends being goofballs to her doing a move that, to me, seems very aggro. "Why do you still have your shirt on? Come on, I'll put sunscreen on you," she orders.

I look at Kim; our eyeballs explode at each other, and I know we are thinking the same thing: *What are we going to do about Macy Whelan?*

I pull off my T-shirt. I have a bathing suit top on, and Macy slathers some SPF 50 on my back and shoulders. I close my eyes, the sun warm on them. I am reminded again how much I love Macy, and I miss her; the pang of missing her overwhelms, with the weight of what happened last night with Max Cooper—so extreme—gnawing at me.

"I'm going to the mainland tomorrow," Macy says as her strong hands slide up, and then across my back; it feels so relaxing, as if this is an actual massage.

"What for?" It occurs to me that Leo will be leaving soon too, for his big family trip to France, and the wind and the world stand still for just a moment.

"Lilly has a doctor appointment, and I'm in charge of getting her there." Macy slaps my back lightly. "You are good to go."

I turn and smile at her, a tight smile filled with worry, trying to be here, present.

Macy leans into me and puts her chin on my shoulder. "I miss you, Moo."

I miss her too. I miss the Macy I knew. This Macy? I'm afraid for her. Maybe I can try to do a one-on-one intervention instead of ambushing her in front of Adera and Kim. I know I would hate it if the three of them came after me about something. "Do you want to sleep over tonight, Mace?"

"I mean. I have to ask; we're getting on the early ferry back to Bay Shore." That's right, she's bringing Lilly to the doctor.

"Hello? Who do you know that gets up at six every day?" I joke, and it makes Macy laugh.

"You sure your *boyfriend* won't mind if I commandeer you for a night?"

No. At this point, even though I only have a few days left with Leo, I need to keep Macy very, very close to me.

* * *

Macy hasn't answered any of my texts, so now I'm at Leo's—well, really, Nate's house; their parents are on the mainland, getting things ready for their big trip to France, which means we're in control. Having a free house is always a big deal; getting to do what we want on our terms is what we wait for all summer. Max Cooper has them all the time, but no one in our friend group has had one yet. I have already jumped up and down on Nate's parents' bed and inhaled the perfume that Leo's mom uses (a Chanel of some kind). I can do whatever I want because there won't be any moms or dads interrupting whatever is happening.

And right now, a lot is happening at the Beckermans'.

The boys from Saltaire are here, hanging out with my friends—not unusual, they're all friends, I get it. Nate is playing *Fortnite* with Benga, Gus, and Max Cooper. I don't want to get into a *Fortnite* vortex, so I'm avoiding the living room, where everything is an off-white something: couch, table, rug, even the vaulted ceilings are painted off-white. Nate's house has a ton of rooms. The living room is the easiest one to hang out in; it has three big shabby-chic-esque couches facing the fireplace, and the mammoth television hangs above the fireplace. The guys have the lights on, and the coffee table is filled with bottles of booze, beer, and other crap. They're pretty lit already, and every so often one of these dummies gets up to take a Snap or use the bathroom. Julian and Ravi are on the deck with Kim and Adera, and they're doing handstands or some nonsense—basically they're all wasted. The only person missing is Macy.

She didn't come to sunset, and when I texted her WYA, she blew me off.

I'm sitting on the deck, looking at my phone, well, scrolling through Insta, when Leo comes out, popcorn in his hand, his hair all shiny, his arms wrapping around me.

"Hey, you wanna go sit in the lifeguard chair?" he asks me, unfortunately not whispering, which means my goofy friends hear exactly what he just said.

Kim and Adera start laughing. "Oooooh, are you going to be *k-i-s-s-i-n-g*?" Adera teases. I give her a playful tap as I stand up.

"Like I said, whipped!" Ravi announces, and Leo laughs.

"You guys are silly," I tell them as I take Leo's hand, walking barefoot onto the beach, the sky above us dark now, the opposite of what we woke up to.

Sitting in the lifeguard chair at night is another thing I like doing in Fire Island; you climb up this short tower, you sit on this bench, and in front of you is the ocean. And it's like you're high above the world, far away from everyone you know.

It takes us three times as long as it normally would to get to the lifeguard chair, because guess what? We stop every twelve heartbeats to make out and rub our faces in each other's necks, and at one point, his fingers get stuck in my hair because I am the worst at brushing the knots out. And as we're about to climb up into the lifeguard chair, we hear a whole bunch of cheering and excitement, and we turn around.

Approaching us is a wild and super-drunk bunch of people, and leading the charge is Macy Whelan as Adera and Kim and Gus and Benga and Shira and Nate and Ravi and Julian are running toward us, all in various states of undress. Then they run past us and jump into the ocean, Macy being the first person in the water, which is just a pitch-black horizon with the occasional whitewater splash. We race up the rungs of the lifeguard chair and sit on the bench and he puts his arms around me.

I'm so glad we get to play lifeguard.

"I was hoping for a little more privacy," Leo whispers.

Macy must have arrived as we left; everyone was Snapping that we were at a free, and obviously she could tell where we're at—I mean Nate's house is iconic. She must have walked over while Leo and I were walking to the lifeguard chair. I'm glad she's with everyone; once we all get back to the house, Macy and I can go home and talk.

And then maybe Macy can go back to being Macy.

"Hey, where'd you go?" Leo whispers, getting my attention. I didn't realize I'd sunk deeply into my head.

"Macy's here," I whisper back, pointing at the water.

"Yeah, well, she's not up here." He laughs.

They're all screeching and splashing in the ocean while Leo and I use this opportunity to lowkey find each other. And then Kim, Macy, and Adera run out of the water laughing and the boys chase them back to the house and it's like they don't even notice us.

"Oh, thank goodness, they're gone," Leo whispers.

We sit in the quiet, searching. It's breezy but not cold, and the sky is clear, and the moon is half-full, and the water looks like a shimmering dark pillow.

●　●　●

My phone starts to buzz, and I pull it out, and it's Adera FaceTiming me. I show Leo the screen with her beautiful face, and he takes the phone out of my hand and answers, "Jasmine Jacobson's phone."

"Leo Burke!!!" Adera announces. "Folks, it's Leo Burke!!!"

Leo laughs and he says, "Yep, it's Leo Burke."

"We're going to a party in Kismet. Wanna come?" Adera is loud, loud and drunk, and Kim is behind her, wet in her bra and underwear, headbanging to a very loud heavy-metal track.

"Nah, we're not going to come to your little party; we're having our own party." Leo laughs.

"What have you done with my girl?"

Leo hands me the phone. "She wants to speak to you."

I laugh, and I take the phone from him. "What up, Adera?" I say, trying to be cool and not really pulling it off.

"You're still with *Leo*?"

"I mean, he's sitting right next to me. You just spoke to him."

"I'm jealous! He's so fine!" Hello, obviously. I know, I want to tell her, *I know he's so fine,* but I don't because I'm shy about admitting to him that I think he is next-level fine, and he's leaning his head back on the chair and not even checking his phone and I guess he's waiting for me to hang up and so I tell Adera I have to go.

"Um, what do you think?" When I hang up, I ask him if he wants to go meet up with everyone.

"One, they're all plastered. I doubt they'll get down the block without falling off the boardwalk. Two, I just want to be alone with you." He pauses. "You know, when I go to France next week—"

"I can barely think about you leaving, Leo," I whisper, interrupting him. "I think your mom gave me shade this morning." I explain what happened when I waved, and he groans.

"I think Emily Burke is very worried I'm going to sulk like I did when I was five being separated from you. I hate it. I hate they're making me go with them." He sighs. "Like, in five days, I have to go away for the rest of the summer." Leo pauses, and he purses his lips and exhales, like all these big thoughts are releasing from his fine body. "And what I want to say to you is this: I don't want you to be with anyone else. When I come home, will you still be my girlfriend?"

"Wait, am I your girlfriend now?" I ask, because, you know, since we're on the topic, I want it basically in writing, and while this isn't exactly writing, it's close to it, I mean the Instagram post of *This is my girl* was kind of in writing, but I haven't even dealt with that one with him yet. I guess I should, though. Ack. So. Much. Is. Happening!

"What? Yes. I mean, yes. I mean, you saw my post and you liked it, so . . ." He smiles, kisses my forehead.

"Um, no. You aren't speaking to me via Instagram. I like those posts, but I'm not going to try to analyze what everything means, cool?" It sounds harsh, but I speak the words as sweetly as I can, and I can see it makes sense to him.

"I'm so dumb. Sorry. I, it's, I've gotten so used to just posting—"

"Isn't there a whole thing where you present a rose or something?" I interrupt him, before he can spin out of control.

And Leo laughs. He gets down on his knees, on the lifeguard platform, and he clasps his hands together and he asks, "Will you be my girlfriend?"

The moonlight forms a halo around Leo, backlighting him, and he is the most beautiful person in the world.

My boyfriend.

*　*　*

As we walk into the house, all that greets us is an eerie silence. Lights are on, in every room—it was apparent to us as we were walking toward it—but no one is here. Half-finished bottles of alcohol are everywhere. Snacks are strewn across the floor. Weed is heavy in the air, but also, the salty breeze of the ocean, some residual boy BO, but our friends are gone. Basically, the only thing those dummies turned off was *Fortnite*. Because of course they did. That's all Nate cares about.

"You think they all went to Kismet?" I ask, hopeful that we are actually alone in a house. Knowing they're all gone is exciting. Knowing there are no adults to crash our moment of alone time is freeing. Knowing that we only have five days left is maddening.

Leo pulls out his phone, texts Nate. I text Macy too; we're supposed to be having a sleepover.

> wya? should I wait for you at Leo's?

Macy doesn't answer me, but Nate hits Leo right away.

"Yahtzee. Yep, they're all there. Which means, we have this whole place to ourselves. Can I show you my room? I have my own room in this house. So . . ." Leo pulls me toward him.

Ah, this, this is a thrill.

"Yes," I say, taking his hand, letting him lead me down the long corridor to where his room is, passing all these other rooms—the Beckermans' office, two bedrooms (one of them smells like ass—Nate's, obviously), lights on in every one of them, and Leo turns around, pulling me toward him, kissing me against a wall, and I don't know what will happen once we are in his bedroom, but I'm so here for it.

"I said, get the fuck off me, dude!"

A voice. Slurring. Interrupting Leo's hand on my thigh, the thigh that's wrapped around his. Leo and I freeze for a moment, and we hear him again.

"I. Can't. Move!" And I know this voice—it's Max Cooper. Why is Max Cooper here? Why isn't he in Kismet with everyone else?

Leo spins, his whole face furrowed, and we run toward the last door in this hallway and into Nate's parents' bedroom, the corner room of this magnificent house, the walls all window, floor to ceiling—it's almost as if the room is floating in the sky with the stars.

And there is Max Cooper, lying on Nate's parents' bed, a bed with navy-blue linen sheets, the lights on above, bright and warm. It smells like beach and weed. Max's hair is all messed up, and his face is etched with panic. At the side of the bed are two bottles of Jack Daniel's and a remote control, flip-flops too.

Atop Max sits Macy Whelan. In her shorts and a T-shirt that says PAVEMENT. Must belong to a dad; it's floating on her body. Her blue eyes are flecked with strain, wild and wide, some vibration emanating that I don't recognize, which makes her seem larger than life, and yet, a wound in a state of festering. She's got him pinned down. He looks so tiny. I remember now: he's not as tall as Leo, or even Macy.

What is she doing to him?

"Burke, get her off me. I can't, I can't, can you get her off me?" Max Cooper slurs, pushing at those lacrosse-trained thighs.

"Macy, what the fuck!" Leo shouts, as he runs to the bed, unsure what to do. He knows he can't put a hand on her, so pushing her off Max Cooper is not an option. And yet we have to help him. We have to help both of them.

I am at Macy's side, and I start to speak, measured and in control. "Macy. Come on. You're hurting him. Is that what you want?" I am really scared, but I know I need to get her out of here. I need to get her on the beach, get some air in her face, get her to find her way back to herself.

"Get away from me!" Macy is fury embodied, her arm raised, her fist in a ball; I don't recognize her.

"Get her off me!" Max slur-yells again.

Leo mutters under his breath, "Shit." He squeezes my hand, and I know, I know he's telling me to keep talking.

"I'm not leaving you here. So can we just, can I take you home?"

"Go play in the sandbox with your new boyfriend and leave me alone!" she snaps.

I put my hand on her shoulder—the shirt is damp from her perspiration, and she shrugs me off. "Come on, Moo, let's go home." We haven't had been good friends to each other in these last few days, but right now, I am her very best friend.

"Max, listen to me," she says, ignoring me.

"No, get the fuck off me!"

Macy's face is now in his, his gold cross dangling in his face, she's that close to him, and he turns away and looks at me, his eyes pleading.

"We are not just friends," she whispers, but because I'm paying very close attention to every flex of every visible muscle in her body, I can hear her. And then she gets up, and Leo is at his side, me at Macy's.

"Jasmine, you should take her home," Leo says, his arm around Max Cooper's shoulder, the two of them on Nate Beckerman's parents' bed.

"Is that a good idea?" Max Cooper asks, and now, now I hear the fear in his voice. Hadn't until this point, but he seems to be sobering up, or resembling some lucidity.

"I don't need you to take me home." Macy says, unsteady in her words as I steer her out of this bedroom, this place, this madness. "I mean, you don't even care about me anymore."

My heart cracks open.

And then she falls into my body.

Her body is an earthquake, a rumble from her toes to the top of her head, her face wet against my neck, the sobs a reverberation, bouncing off the walls of this house.

"Let me take you home, cool?" I tell her.

"Just me and you?" she asks, softening.

"Just me and you."

•   •   •

Macy is unleashing, much steadier now, yelling at the universe as we walk along the beach, from Holly to Birch, just a few staircases back to what home is for her. So much has gone wrong for us. So much. But it's much worse for her. All in real time, right before my eyes.

"How could you humiliate me like that?" she asks, her eyes wild, her hair blowing in the wind, her arms flailing. I'm counting the staircases, counting them down, to Birch. Nate's house is on Holly; we passed Oak and Pine, and we're coming across the wraparound staircase of Broadway. We're halfway to Birch, and I'm just holding my breath that we get there. It's warm and dark out here, the only light from above, the moonlight, and the warm glow of houses, where people are still awake.

"I was trying to stop you from whatever you were doing to Max Cooper!" And now, now the adrenaline of everything that happened hits me, and I want her to be okay and I want to go back to Leo, but I know that I need to make sure she's home, and not stalking Max Cooper.

"Stop me from what? All I was trying to do was make things right between us." Macy spits it all out, in a rush, all the words coming out of her. "I honestly thought he wanted me there."

I'm not sure how the scenario really played out, but I know that he didn't want her on top of him. She stops walking, just as we're getting to Cranberry. One more little stretch of sand until we hit Birch, and I can get her home.

"He is *not* interested in you. You get that, right? Also, he has a girlfriend . . ."

"And where the fuck is she? Huh? Newsflash, I'm the one that's here. I'm the one who wants to be with him!" Macy yells.

"But he said *no*!" I can't believe I am having to say these words out loud. "Macy. Stop. Look at me. Just imagine this. If I were lying on Nate's parents' bed and woke up and found a guy straddling me? Do you hear me? Do you see why what you were doing was not okay?"

Macy's eyes are wet with this trauma, this sadness that's engulfed her. "Moo. Maybe we should go back and see if he's okay. He looked upset."

"Macy. You can't go near him ever again." I enunciate each word, and every word hurts to say, knowing I am literally ending us too.

Macy lunges at me, and my insides flinch. I can't believe Macy would try to hurt me too. She grasps at my shoulders, her breath a hot mess of alcohol and cigarettes, her nails digging into my skin. "Take that back."

"Maybe it's a good thing you are leaving tomorrow, Mace."

Her face falls, even further, into something lost. She spins on her heel, bursts into a sprint, knowing she can outrun me. And she's getting farther and farther away, almost disappearing into the blackness that is this beach as she charges toward Birch.

"Macy! Wait!"

I race—well, as much as you can in the sand—to Birch, bound up the stairs to her house, which is enveloped in the darkness of sleep, except for the light on the porch. I try to open the door, and it's locked.

If it's locked, it must mean Macy is home.

She's locked me out of her house?

> Macy, I'm at your door. Let me in.

No answer.

> Macy, I love you. Please let me in.

> Stay away from me.

Stay away from me. She told Alice Adams to stay away from me, and now she's telling me to stay away from her.

I don't realize I'm crying until I'm almost back at Nate's house.

●　●　●

The house is still empty, but the lights are no longer on in every room, and the living room and kitchen are spotless. Every fiber of me aches, my throat parched. Have I been gone for that long? I look at my phone: it's 2:22 a.m. Leo has cleaned this whole place up in the time that I've been away, and now he is asleep on the couch, lying on his back, his hands folded on his chest.

I do the only thing I can think of: I wake him.

"Can I lie here next to you?" I whisper, and he holds out his arms, moving over, welcoming me into them.

The Next Day

Chapter Seven

My phone is blowing up.

I lift my head off my pillow and look at it; it's 8:08 a.m.

SHIT.

I'm late for work. Which means Sue has been calling me, wanting to know where I am. I have never been late to work at Crabby's, not so far this summer, and not last summer. I call Sue and apologize; maybe she can hear something broken inside, but she doesn't yell, she just tells me to hurry up.

I sit up, my body worn-out.

Stay away from me.

And I start crying.

And of all the things to wake Mom up, it's that, the silent sound of tears falling down my face; Mom has that super-sonic mom hearing, the one that knows when I start the day in a spiral.

"Jazzy?" she asks, and in a blink she is sitting beside me, her arms around me as I cry and she shushes me into consolation. It takes a few minutes for me to catch my breath and have some control over my tear ducts.

"Mom," I start, so tentatively. It's too early to start the day off this heavy. But I can't stop talking. "Mom. Macy. She's just. I don't know. It was so awful." I'm not making sense, and I understand why: I can barely understand what happened last night.

"I was expecting to see her lying next to you when I went to the bathroom last night. So I'm guessing she didn't make it?" Mom asks.

"No. Mom. Worse. She . . . she kind of pinned Max Cooper down and we had to pull her off and then she told me to stay away from her," I say, barely holding the ugly cry at bay, obviously giving her the abridged edition.

Mom releases me from her safety-net hold, and she is in mom-to-the-rescue mode, measured and careful as she watches me. "Where is Macy now?"

"She's taking Lilly to the mainland." I look at the time on my phone. It's almost eight thirty. They're probably gone by now. "Mom. I didn't even recognize her, you know? She was like some other person."

"Oh, honey. I imagine that there is a lot about Macy that is hidden from you." She pauses. "But the important thing is that you were able to help her, and help Max too."

I was able to help Max Cooper.

My phone buzzes again, and it's Sue, wya-ing me. I hold the phone out to Mom, and she rolls her eyes. "She's a nuisance, that one."

And today, today I won't have time to do *Galentines*, and in addition to all the other things ailing my heart, now I have that stress.

Today is going to be a very long day.

* * *

I stumble into Crabby's, not because I'm overtired—technically, I've had almost four hours' sleep, so not bad—but because my brain is addled, stuffed with seeing Macy holding Max Cooper hostage, his gold cross dangling from her neck.

"Jazz?" Sue asks as I grab the sanitizer and start wiping down the counter, enjoying the rhythmic motion of the back and forth of it all. "You look—"

"I know," I snap and immediately feel bad about it. Sue hasn't done anything wrong, she's just doing her job. "Sorry," I say immediately as I turn to face her. "I had a rough night."

"I had plenty of those when I was your age too." She laughs.

There is a lot that Sue doesn't know about me either; she doesn't know I prefer weed over booze, and she doesn't know that I have never had actual sex, and she doesn't know that sometimes, when she's not looking, I will sneak-eat a mini peppermint patty. But she does know when I'm off-kilter, and she does know how to back off.

And I appreciate that about her.

• • •

KIM: Did you do the intervention without us

ADERA: Jazz, we're hearing some heavy shit.

KIM: spill the tea

KIM: ???

ADERA: Jazzy?

KIM: ?

ADERA: Come by Birch, okay?

kk

The thing is, I don't know how to talk to my friends right now. The only person I'd like to speak to is the one who told me to stay away from her.

• • •

Leo and Max Cooper are waiting for me after work at the dock, eating ice cream cones they've just purchased from me. The image of Max Cooper lying on that bed—flat-out drunk with Macy sitting on him—I haven't been able to unsee it. This drama, it rolled deep, extending into everyone's lives. I have been replaying the last two weeks over and over in my head. How I knew Macy wasn't really over Max Cooper, but not realizing how deeply wounded she'd been and how far she was capable of going.

Leo wraps himself around my dumb sticky body, and I accept the salve that is Leo Burke.

"Break it up, break it up," Max Cooper jokes.

"You wanna ride to Dunewood Bay?" I suggest.

Because we have to talk, and I don't want to do it here, in town, or on Birch, where our friends are. I want to go somewhere where we won't get interrupted, and that's Dunewood, the next town over, in the opposite direction of Saltaire.

"How about we ride down to the nude beach instead?" he answers, because he's incorrigible.

I roll my eyes at him.

"Oh, just kidding. How about we just follow you?"

Dunewood Bay is the most remote of our bays here; you have to trudge through a little bit of sand and brush to get to it, but once you do, it's magnificent, an expansive view of the bay, without any little kids running around squealing because there isn't a playground for them to make their aforementioned noise. So it's tranquil, and it's almost hidden away from the sleepy town.

Leo and Max Cooper follow me, and we leave our bikes flat in the tall grass and walk along the sand toward the shoreline, avoiding the humans who are enjoying the Dunewood Bay, only a few of them, here too for the privacy (so there is some topless lady action happening). We sit in the sand, flat on our butts, no towels. It's sunny today, not too hot, and I raise my face to the sky.

"How you doing, Jazz?" Max Cooper asks, and I can't believe he is asking me how I'm doing when it's him I'm concerned about.

I start and then I stop, the floodgate of tears about to burst, and I have to stop talking, or else the crying will begin again. I'm wobbly, and Leo nods, an assurance that I can do this, I can be here with my boyfriend and with Max Cooper. I want to say, *I've spent my whole sophomore year waiting to be here with Macy for the summer, and instead, I'm finding out that my best friend is not well, and that she hurt you, and, oh, I have a boyfriend,* but instead I say, "I'm wondering how *you're* doing, Max."

But seriously, Max Cooper's face right now, it's a redefining of an ugly cry. "I wanted to say thanks, Jazz."

The world goes soft around me, and I moan, "Oh, Max." Leo is alarmed by how my voice cracks, and he rubs my back, in little soft circles.

Max looks at me, his face contorted with something terrible, something sad. I turn away toward the bay and watch the soft ebb of the water pulsing toward the sand and I kind of wish it would swoop me away, away from all of what he's about to tell me. I don't wipe the tears silently falling down my face.

"I can't tell you how many times I've looked out my window and she's been there, just been there, waiting. Texting. All the texting. Even though I kept telling her I just wanted to be friends."

I know now what the waiting really was, because I've been there waiting for him too, not realizing I was enabling Macy. That we all were, anytime she veered off onto his walk, rode to his house, and stared at her phone, while Adera, Kim, whoever was there, was waiting for *her* to snap out of it.

"You know, we came into Fair Harbor because I actually wanted to talk to you. Remember? Tell you about all this shit that was happening. Because I figured you really didn't know what she was doing."

He is correct. I didn't know the full extent of it. I didn't tally up all the incidents. The riding into Saltaire, into town, sitting in the gazebo, not realizing it was because she was waiting to see him ride his bike by. And I certainly had no idea about any of its impact on him.

"You should have seen her on the ferry, dude. She kept looking at me and taking pictures, and it was *freaky*. I had to go downstairs so I could get away from her." Max Cooper's face prunes up again, the lines of fear and *Fortnite* permanently plastered.

"Wait, she told me you were, like, connecting on the ferry," I tell him.

"Nah, dude. I was sitting a few rows in front of her; I didn't even see her waiting for the ferry at Bay Shore. I was probably the first person on? Anyway, she rocks up to me, and is like, 'Hey,' and I'm like, 'Hey,' and that was it. Then she asks if we can get a selfie, and I'm like, 'Nah, dude,' cuz you know, I don't want anything on Insta—my girl sees that and it's drama for me. And I told her that, and she laughed, and I was like, *Okay, we're cool.* That was it, Jazz."

I don't say a word. There aren't any in my head, the words are all lodged in my heart, palpitating there. That wasn't how Macy described their ferry ride.

"You have to believe me when I tell you that I did not want this to happen to Macy. I'm not a jerk. I told her last summer I didn't want to hook up ever again. I just wanted to be friends. I thought we were cool. Even this summer, I was clear with her that, like, I still didn't want to. That I have a girl." Max's knees have been up this whole time, and now he hugs them close to his body and hangs his head in that space. He is definitely crying. I don't put my hand on his back. I want to hold Max Cooper, the way Mom held me this morning, but I know I just need to wait for him to gather himself. He's not this evil demon. He's like me, trying to figure it out, in the moment, all the time.

"These last few weeks have not been normal. Not in any way," I finally say, my voice continuing to crack, all the emotion of this wrestling to be released.

Leo nuzzles his nose in my neck. "You okay, baby?"

Oh, my heart! It's the first time Leo's referred to me as "baby." Another milestone for me and Leo. I nod and whisper, "Thanks," to my boyfriend.

"I heard she's off-island," Max Cooper says.

"Yeah. She took her grandmother to the doctor." I'm not mad at Max Cooper anymore. Or Max. I can call him just plain Max. He feels bad for everything that happened to Macy; he actually feels something about what happened between him and Macy, something dark, something real, something regretful, something heavy, something fathoms more painful than I gave him credit for. "I don't know when she's coming back, though. Have you told your parents?"

"What? No. I haven't even told Evan. But I did get to sleep in Burke's bed, so, winning."

We all laugh, for the first time, and it feels natural—a catharsis.

"Look. You saved us both, Jazz, and I appreciate you doing that." I look at him, look into his eyes, see how much he means what he is saying, how much pain he is in.

Mom said the same thing this morning to me: I saved them both. One interruption changed the balance of these two people, one of whom I love very much, despite all the wrong in the ether of her. I can feel the tears hanging out behind my eyeballs, so I don't speak, because if I do, I will not be making sentences, only pathetic sounds. Leo strokes my leg, not a hot stroke, a stroke of concern, care, and love, and I lean on my boyfriend's shoulder.

And the weight, the residual gravity of it, that has had its grip on my throat for weeks, it evaporates. Gone. And, for the first time ever, I have empathy for Max.

Imagine that. Max fucking Cooper making me feel better.

• • •

ADERA: wya

with MAX COOPER

KIM: ???

idek anymore

• • •

I opt not to go to sunset. I'm not in the mood for the whole crew, to have to explain to them why Macy is off-island. Adera and Kim are already suspicious. I can't even imagine what they've heard, if anything, really. All that might be public knowledge is that Max woke up in Leo's bed, and Leo slept in his parents' bedroom.

And so, instead, Leo and I hang out in my house, far, far away from anyone that wants me to stay away from them, and every time I stray into seeing what I can't unsee, I squeeze Leo's leg and he distracts me with his beautiful dimples, accompanied by some nerdy photographer fact.

It's going to be a long summer without him, without her.

The Day before Leo Leaves

Epilogue

It's six a.m., and my body is vibrating with this thing I'm feeling, of having Leo as my boyfriend. I take my outdoor shower and I sing his name in my head. I put on my hoodie and I realize it's his. I look at my phone and he's there, on it, my phone wallpaper, my heart, everywhere. This morning is strangely cool for July, and I'm ready for it as I strap my gear on my shoulder. I'm on cruise control, only a day left with Leo before he goes on this family trip, barreling down the stairs to the beach, which is almost all empty, with the sky a brilliant shade of blue and little puddles of marshmallow clouds, and the air crisp, and there he is in the center of it all.

My boyfriend.

Tomorrow, Leo leaves for the mainland, and from there, he will go to France for six weeks. It scares me a little, to be apart after finding each other, these feelings that are all swirling around, not just in my head, but my stomach and my knees, and I feel him, like, under my skin.

A wave engulfs me; to see him is to feel for the first time like my eyes are wide open, what my world looks like with Leo in it. That rush of Leo, standing in the sand, facing the ocean, his Leica in his hands, his eye searching for a shot, and I call out to him and he turns and his smile is more than everything, it's the *only* thing.

He's wearing jeans too and a blue hoodie, it's only partially zipped up and I can see he's not wearing a shirt underneath, and the same thrill as always races through me, this invitation into my imagination, of what has been and what will be.

"You sure you don't want to leave the Hasselblad or the Leica with me when you go to France?" I put my arms around his waist, his arms wrap around my shoulders, our cameras dangling as we meld, meld as deeply as two clothed humans on a windy beach can.

"Is that all you want from me, Jasmine?" Leo laughs, kissing my neck.

I want you to spend the summer with me, I want to tell him. Instead, I tell him something quiet and personal, something that makes him smile, something that belongs to us.

* * *

Our morning ritual this week—after a jaunt in the lifeguard chair and my fifty frames—is to come back to my house together and upload. I like having his eye on my frames; he sometimes sees the things I don't, like today, the way the light plays off the calm veneer of the ocean, whereas all I saw was a dull landscape, trying to capture the emptiness I feel in the wake of Macy returning to the mainland.

And so it's a shot of the horizon, emptiness ahead, beauty surrounding it, the perspective clear.

> **Yeah, I've Been Missing You.**
> #ariana #galentines #supportwomen #photography
> #summerproject

For Macy, obviously.

I haven't heard from her since she told me to stay away from her. Right now, she's in Philadelphia, with Olive, far, far away from Fire Island, an ache in my heart.

• • •

I get hit with a wave of panic; this has been happening all week—between Macy leaving and Leo leaving soon, it's a lot—and I reach out to the counter to catch my breath. Woozy is not cute. I drink some water and try to talk myself through this little flourish I'm having; the nerves have really found their way to lodging themselves within.

Sue has told us that our third person starts tomorrow, which is a huge relief. I'm taking the day off so that I can begin it with Leo and spend every possible second with him until he boards the ferry.

I didn't have that choice, to say goodbye to Macy when she left Fair Harbor, the day after what happened at Nate's house. And maybe the day after tomorrow, when Leo's gone, I'll feel the full effect of her absence, but for now, for now, I am going to push all of that out of my mind.

"Excuse me, hon, can I get a Rocky Road on a sugar cone, chocolate sprinkles, please?" It's my mom who breaks this haze.

"Oh, hey, Mom."

"You look a little janky." Mom's hair is loose, and it looks like she's actually brushed it today, which is rare for her during the summer.

"I just need to drink some water." I demonstrate the drinking of the water, and she laughs.

"How you doing? Hear from Macy?" Mom asks.

I look at my phone. "No. Not yet." I bite my lip, the tears in my eyes; it's like I have a new access to my emotions, all access, and I'm here to tell you I am not into it.

Stay away.

"Well. She'll come around, you'll see." Mom smiles. "Aww, honey, don't cry."

"Mom, it's like I can't stop," I say, wiping a tear away, trying to hold the dam of them back. "I get so, so sad about Macy. And even Max, what happened with him."

Mom turns her head to see if there are any customers behind her. There aren't. It's a miracle, but there is no one tugging at my nerves for their ice cream cones, and then she leans to my side and calls out to Sue, "Sue, can Jazzy take her break now?"

Sue who has been watching me break down at least eight times a day these last few days, nods, her arms folded across her chest, her hair pulled back from her face, all those beads of sweat lingering.

I mutter, "Thanks," as I take my apron off and leave Crabby's.

I don't need much from Mom, but right now, I'll take whatever she's offering.

*   *   *

Mom and I walk to the end of the dock and sit on a bench, each of us with our bottle of water.

"Can I get a kiss?" Mom says, breaking the ice, I guess.

"Mom, stop being thirsty." I laugh while crying at the same time.

"I just want to say this one thing . . ." Mom starts.

"Is this going to be about Macy? Because, like, I really can't, Mom."

"Yes. Listen, this one thing, I've been thinking about it. I think it might help you as you . . . figure things out."

"Mom, I am perfectly capable of doing that on my own. I mean, Mom, come on," I protest.

"I know. But, just, just listen. You know, Macy spends a lot of her time thinking about ways to win, strategies and tactics that create scenarios where she succeeds. It's her training as an athlete. But it does not work in matters of the heart. Macy didn't have a mutual and consenting relationship with Max. She was obsessed with him. You understand? Max just wanted to be friends. So what happened? She spent all year coming up with another strategy to get him to like her. She approached Max the way she approached a match or whatever it's called. And she kept losing."

Something clicks within. Macy never stopped liking Max Cooper, and she came back to Fair Harbor, approaching him like she would a lacrosse meet: with a game plan.

Mom is annoying a lot of the time, but when I need her, she knows how to have my back, by being the Yoda of moms with her way of getting it.

• • •

I'm waiting for Leo to change into his wet suit, he's taking forever, so I'm sitting on the couch in his living room, teenagers and adults all floating around me. I'm pretending to be deeply engrossed in my Instagram feed, but it's not working; every time someone whirls by me, I look up, hoping it's Leo, who is still in his room, putting his wet suit on. I can hear him, his voice a little raised, his mother yelling at him, and I wonder what's happening, why they're fighting; her yelling at him reminds me that really, there is no such thing as a cool mom—they're all a little bit kooky and cranky and if you're lucky, a little cool, but never completely and wholly cool.

Nate and his dad, Rob, plant themselves on either side of me, like they're conspiring to torture me, and then Nate's dad asks me how my summer is coming along and Nate snorts.

"What?" Rob says. Rob is bald and is so blind, he wears Coke-bottle-thick lenses in his glasses and he is the first dad I ever met who is furry in that way that you're like, *Do all men grow hair everywhere?* (The answer, I learned from Mom, is: not all men.)

"Dad, seriously. Where have you been?" Nate says in his Scottish burr, those *r*s really catching in his throat.

"Here?" Rob is perplexed and I guess he doesn't know about me and Leo and I'm not up for getting into it with a dad.

I turn to Nate. "Why is Leo's mom yelling at him?"

Nate shrugs, but I can tell he knows what's up.

"Emily is worried about her son and his new girlfriend," Rob says slyly, as he puts his arm around me and squeezes playfully.

Oh, so Rob does know about me and Leo, but I don't get to pursue the line of questioning because Nate jumps up and groans, *"Dad!"* in his regular voice and pulls me up and away from any of the adult Beckermans and Burkes that might be lurking.

Clearly, I don't belong in the house.

● ● ●

Leo is cranky. He storms out onto the deck, but slows down the moment he sees me leaning against the rails, taking photos of Nate being a goof, and Leo gives me a big, long, emotional hug, his hands all up in my hair and his body rigid.

"Sorry," he murmurs.

"I understand. I've got a mom too," I whisper. "What were you fighting about?"

"We were fighting because I don't want to go with them to France. And she is just not listening to me," Leo says, exasperated.

"It's only six weeks," I say, the refrain we keep telling each other when one of us starts freaking about being apart, which has been happening more and more as tomorrow approaches. "We are going to FaceTime every day . . ."

"I know, I know, Jasmine, but, like, I can't even imagine not touching . . ."

Nate interrupts us with a whistle blow. "The waves wait for no man or woman," he announces, anxious to get to his precious waves, ready in his wet suit and white sunscreen slathered on his nose.

Even though their house is on the oceanfront, you cannot just walk to the ocean from the house; because of seashore erosion, there are dunes to ward off further damage; ergo, we have to walk out of the house, onto Holly, up the stairs, across the walkway that hovers above the dunes, and onto the beach. In all ways, Fire Island is an outer barrier island, protecting the mainland of the south shore of Long Island from the ocean. Whatever.

Leo has one hand in mine, his surfboard under his other arm, as we walk, Nate chattering about nothing in general, Leo rather silent, and I see Adera, standing on the stairs at the end of their walk on Holly, looking out into the ocean. Like she's been waiting for us.

"Whatcha up to?" I ask Adera. She's got big blue square sunglasses on, a white bikini top, and a white crocheted coverall, her hair pulled back, she looks so beautiful, I really want to take her portrait but right now, I'm going to be shooting my boyfriend and his cousin on their surfboards.

"Expanding my horizons." Adera is so deadpan it's hilarious, and I tap her hand gently and tell her to come with us.

Leo kisses me before he and his surfboard head into the ocean, with Nate giving me mock air kisses. I turn to see if the moms are watching, and sure enough, there they are, Emily and Sandy standing on their deck, arms folded across their chests, watching us, their faces looking like I'm some secret agent from vagina-land. I wave at them, and smile. I don't care that they will not wave back; I'm not going to be intimidated by moms. I have my own mom, thank you very much, and she's a handful.

"You still haven't heard from her?" Adera asks. It's been almost a week now since she's left, and she hasn't returned. And in the last few days, I've been tiptoeing around Snaps, hoping she'll open mine, hoping we can talk, even if it means closure.

Stay away from me.

"No." I haven't ever felt this brokenhearted, ever; the silence of Macy is unbearable.

"Let's send her a Snap and see if she opens it," Adera suggests.

We do just that, the sun in front of us, so we get the best and warmest of lights, and we caption it, We Miss You!

And then we stare at the phone for a minute, waiting to see if she opens it.

She doesn't.

"Well, maybe she will, later," Adera offers. She squeezes my hand. "You know, that dummy Max is right. You getting in there? You saved them both."

"I appreciate you saying that." I exhale. I haven't been able to talk about the details of that night at all, other than with Leo. It feels good to touch upon it, as much as I possibly can, which I know, I am not ready to speak to every detail; it's a trauma, frozen in time. "You should have seen her, Adera, like, she just, she was somewhere else, you know, in her head. It made me think of all these times when she kind of snapped at someone or even last summer, when she wouldn't come out at all, and when she did, she seemed so . . . out of it." I start tearing up again.

Adera puts her arm around me, and I lean into her. "Well. You showed up for her. You got her off that dude. Like, if you hadn't, we'd be dealing with some other bullshit."

I nod. I look out toward the ocean. The waves are almost nonexistent, and the sand is a little damp, but my boyfriend and his cousin don't care; they're having so much fun.

"And look. You got a boyfriend now. And even though you're going to have to do a little long distance, you're gonna be able to FaceTime him and stuff." She pauses. "Have you . . . you know, yet?"

Yep. Adera is asking about *s-e-x*. And for all my talking about how I think about it all day long, now, now I feel very shy and protective about whatever is happening between me and Leo, or whatever we've explored so far. "Um. No."

"Well, girl, guess what? That boy is going to be jumping out of his skin to get home to you." She laughs, that great big smile of hers warming every part of my Macy-sad heart.

I turn my camera to her, take a photo. I look at the shot and sigh. It's basically perfect, with her pink-glossy lips curled upward, a slight sinister snarl, those endless pools of eyes peeking over the top edge of her sunglasses, her hair gelled and pulled taut—all there is is her face. "The camera loves you, Adera, it really does."

* * *

Macy opens our Snap.

She doesn't respond.

Still, it's progress. And one of these days, she will open it and Snap back at me.

* * *

I've been talking about the inflatable boat that is in the shed for a few days, how nice it is to just hang out in it and float around, and Leo wants to do that, right now, before everyone shows up for dinner. Leo and I go into the shed and pull out the air pump and the flattened inflatable boat and we bring everything out to the front of the house, to where our little beach is, where the sand meets the bay, and fifteen minutes later, this rubber boat is in perfect shape to go floating. Leo lifts it over the ratty and short picket fence that lines our house, the line of demarcation being the sand, the water being open to the public walking by. I step into the boat, the water lapping at my toes, and it feels great, and Leo pulls the boat out on to the water a bit and then he gets in and we have our legs in each other's laps and I lean my head back as Leo paddles and talks to me and I take off my shirt but I have my bikini top on and it's possible a boob slips out but I adjust myself so quickly that I'm back to being an awkward ding-dong and Leo says, "Oh, come on," so I guess I did flash him, and I splash some water at my McDimple. "Perv," I say, but, oh, I would have loved to have just taken it all off, just to see his expression again, that look of pleasure that washes over his face whenever our lips come together and that smile of his, and the way he is looking at me right now, I will carry it with me always, and I settle in Leo's body with my legs thrown over his, watching him paddle, the way he glides us along, the way his arms expand and contract, the way his skin glistens in the darkening sunlight, and I think about how much I love summer.

Acknowledgments

Fire Island is a real magical sandbar of serenity, and its remoteness has been a salve to my soul; I've ridden my bike up and down its walks for so long, they are etched in my breath.

As a writer, you envision your world. Maybe even a plot. Fill it with characters who you follow as their story unfolds.

But a book is not truly formed without a team of brilliant visionaries, and I say thank you, thank you, thank you to every person who said yes every step of the way; you define kindness.

Christopher Schelling, my literary agent, my friend, my champion. If not for Christopher seeing what was possible, this book in your hands would still be sitting in a folder on my laptop, right beside my teen girl vampire detective novel. I am so thankful, every day, to know you.

Ari Lewin, who saw Jazz and turned her into song. Thank you for giving us a chance to be seen.

Thank you to Elise LeMassena and Jennifer Klonsky for this moment, for your steadfast and enthusiastic belief in *Getting Over Max Cooper*, for making this real—oh, I am forever grateful. Thank you Mallory Heyer and Theresa Evangelista for this beautiful cover. Thank you to every single person at G. P. Putnam's Sons, from launch to this very second, for getting behind *GOMC*.

Thank you to Tori Chickering, my dear friend, for giving me the title to my beloved book. Thank you to the women who wrote the blurbs: Jennifer Mathieu, Dante Medema, Emmy Laybourne, and Lisi Harrison. And oh hi, Jeff Bishop, you're cool.

I am also so grateful to my friends and family, who make it possible for me to feel loved and who take care of me up close and from afar. You all know who you are; I love you so.

Thank you to the UWS Irving Farm, which is where I first wrote *Getting Over Max Cooper* in those scary months when I was first unemployed, grieving the loss of my dad. You have terrible Wi-Fi, which is why I was able to write instead of trolling OKCupid for a bashert.

Earlier in my life, my best friend took hers; I had no idea the tremors reverberating below. I missed so much. This book is written in her memory.

Finally, to the two most important women in my orbit. To my mother, Shula Karp: hey, Ma, your Instagram game is fire! And to my daughter, Ruby Karp: how lucky I am, every day, to be in your presence (and yes, FaceTime counts).